The classical theme of pure beings fighting the forces of evil and chaos is handled deftly, with a believable character and a misty, faraway setting. . . . The novel's success rests upon the author's ability to portray both a human girl and mythological beings with dignity. *Library Journal*

Dramatic use of tension carries the plot swiftly forward. . . . Though Christian precepts clearly underscore the story, they do not intrude. Imaginative and entertaining.
The American Library Association Booklist

A delightful new fantasy of journey and quest . . . Madeleine L'Engle, C.S. Lewis, Dr. Tolkien, meet Robert Siegel. He may be moving into your select circle.
The Episcopalian

Alpha Centauri bursts in the sky like the Fourth of July, brilliant to behold. High adventure, drama, self-sacrifice, courage, a bit of romance—it is all to be found in this well-written and beautifully illustrated tale. This is a fine work and a joy to recommend. Books like this don't come along very often. *Christianity Today*

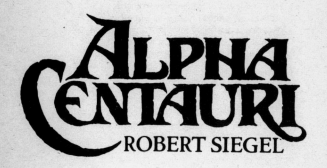

ALPHA CENTAURI

ROBERT SIEGEL

BERKLEY BOOKS, NEW YORK

This Berkley book contains the complete
text of the original hardcover edition.
It has been completely reset in a type face
designed for easy reading, and was printed
from new film.

ALPHA CENTAURI

A Berkley Book / published by arrangement with
Cornerstone Books

PRINTING HISTORY
Cornerstone Books edition published 1980
Berkley trade paperback edition / October 1982

Maps by Robbin Cadena.

ISBN: 0-425-05708-9

A BERKLEY BOOK ® TM 757,375
Berkley Books are published by Berkley Publishing Corporation,
200 Madison Avenue, New York, New York 10016.
The name "BERKLEY" and the stylized "B" with design are trademarks
belonging to Berkley Publishing Corporation.
PRINTED IN THE UNITED STATES OF AMERICA

For Lenaye
Lucy
& Christy

May stone open
star beckon
& heart sing

until you are home at last.

Contents

Alpha Centauri

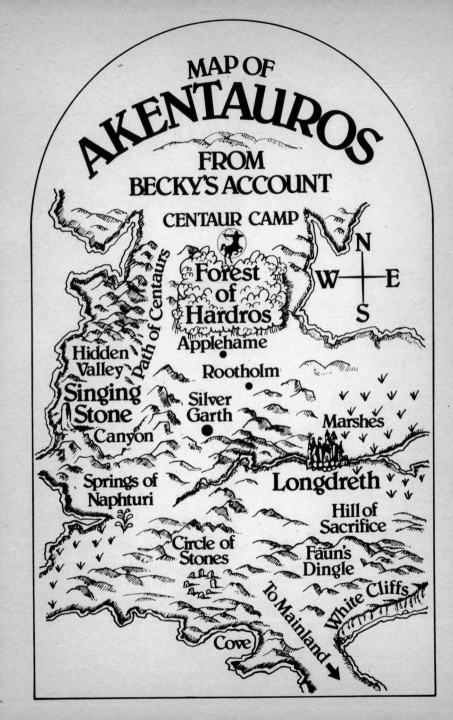

· *Canters* ·

As their headlights rose and fell on the fog, Becky strained to see beyond the edge of the road. It was an hour since they'd dropped down off the motorway into pockets of fog, which soon spread to a blanket. The glittering cat's-eye markers were missing from the roadside, and only an occasional ghostly tree or fence showed they were still on course.

Two hours ago they had left London for the wilds of Surrey. The suddenness with which the English landscape changed was exciting to an American. One moment you were in the heart of a modern city and almost the next in country that looked as it had hundreds, perhaps thousands, of years ago. Especially in the fog! Becky flinched a little as an enormous black limb reached out for her. Things didn't look the same in the fog. Trees swept by in grotesque postures. Hills and houses stared sinisterly at their passing car. At times the car seemed to float in an ocean which cast up before it shapes and faces from the depths of time.

She was glad when her father broke the silence: "I hope Charlie leaves the lights on, or we'll miss the place." Charlie was an old friend of her father's, a fellow American who had settled in Surrey years back. She'd met him briefly in London. A month ago, Charlie had asked them down to his farm for this weekend, but since then they'd heard nothing from him.

"Canters," she said to herself, repeating the strange address like a charm, "Canters, Dunsfold, Godalming, Surrey." Becky was from Massachusetts, and for her, English addresses held a magic old as the rhymes about St. Ives and Banbury Cross. Her father, a history professor visiting the University of London, had suggested she join him. The principal of her junior high had agreed—reluctantly, since he feared her math would suffer. Becky was overjoyed, for she hated math as much as she loved to read. Her father bought her two richly illustrated books to take along, one on Queen Elizabeth I and another called *Mysteries of Ancient Europe*. These she read and dreamed over for weeks before the silver jet rose above the blue Atlantic.

She liked London, especially the famous Tower, which she'd already visited twice. Her favorite room was that in which Lady Jane Grey kept a vigil all night before going to the block. Lady Jane had been only seventeen and could speak five languages. She was terribly brave. Becky also liked the wax figures at Madame Tussaud's. Yet now and then she felt homesick for the brilliant reds and yellows of the Massachusetts fall. She missed her large sable collie, Hrothgar, and sometimes even her sisters.

"Why is it called 'Canters'?" she asked.

"I don't know," her father replied. "Perhaps because horses canter—Charlie loves horses. We may get a chance to do some riding." Just then two fuzzy spots of light swung into view. Her father braked and turned the wheel. "I think this is the right gate."

The car bounced up a narrow lane between two gatelamps. From one hung a white signboard carved like a horse on which *Canters* shone in black. Fences on both sides widened to a yard where an amber light glowed through the fog. It was the courtyard of an old farm; the dark outline of house and barns formed three sides of a cobbled square. As they stopped, the figure of a man appeared in a yellow doorway. A moment later a red face with flashing teeth poked in her window.

"Well, Fred, you're here! And Becky! Just in time to give Rebecca her hot mash. Welcome to Canters! How was the trip down?" He spoke in a loud voice and, without waiting for an answer, ran around the car to shake her father's hand.

"Just fine, Charlie," her father started to reply, but was interrupted by a high, impatient whinny.

Charlie laughed. "The old girl's hungry." He wore a tweed cap, red-checked shirt, and khaki pants tucked in high rubber boots—"Wellingtons" they called them here. The big man turned and the two followed him through the yellow doorway into the warm smells of a stable. It consisted of three stalls, one occupied by a white horse with a yellowish tail.

"Becky, meet Rebecca!" Charlie patted rippling withers. The mare turned and nodded in Becky's direction, twitching an ear.

"Hi, Rebecca," she replied, placing one hand gingerly on the horse's glossy shoulder. She'd never liked the name "Rebecca," especially when her parents said it in a certain tone, but it seemed right at home on the large mare. One black eye rolled at her, showing the white. One hoof stamped. Charlie was busy grooming the other side. He and her father talked for a minute about the drive down, then her father left for the house. Rebecca stamped again.

"Just a minute, old girl. First the blanket, *then* the mash. Here, give this to her, but watch your fingers." He handed Becky something like a piece of dry dog food, only larger. "It's a horse nut," he explained. Holding her palm flat, she lifted the treat toward the quivering nose. Rebecca opened her lips, baring yellowish teeth, and took it at one nod. Her lips felt warm and rough.

Charlie laughed, "Sucks it up like an old Hoover, doesn't she? See that?" He held up a blunt forefinger. "A pony took the tip off that going for a cube of sugar." He laughed again, louder.

Rebecca nipped at Becky's shirtpocket, looking for more, then blew out her lips at her ear, "Nh-Nh-Nh-Nh-Nh-*NH!*" Her warm breath tickled.

"She likes you." Charlie handed her another horse nut.

"How old is she?" the girl asked, holding it out to the horse.

"That's one secret a lady'll take to her grave, my grandmother used to say. But I'd guess she's close to twenty. Her father was in the Coronation."

"Do you have others?" Becky looked at the two empty stalls.

"Just the ponies, Dikkon and Piccolo. But they're gone for the weekend to the Godalming School for the Handicapped. They're wonderful with kids who've never had a chance to ride."

"What colors are they?"

"Dikkon is gray, and Piccolo black as night. She's the one who mistook my finger for sugar." He held it up again. "She's a Connemara, and lively as they come. But Dikkon's cleverer. He opens gates—and doors. One morning I found him in the dining room eating oranges out of a bowl with never a 'please' or 'thank you.' I wrote it up for the local paper. Horses are like people, when you get to know 'em."

Still talking, Charlie threw a blanket over the horse and attached a bag of steaming bran behind her ears. Rebecca settled down to steady munching. The whole stable had a comfortable smell, Becky thought, watching Charlie fork clean straw. She wondered what it was like to sleep here.

From the other side of the wall came a songlike moan. "That'll be Marigold," Charlie said, looking up from the straw. "She has twin calves, Honey and Perriwinkle. Here, let me show you!" He stuck the fork in a bale and led her through a shabby door. The golden Jerseys stared sleepily over three pink noses, sulky at being disturbed. The calves' expressions were so much like the mother's, Becky laughed out loud.

"Very respectable people, cows!" Charlie touched his cap. Then he threw a switch and guided her out into the gray yard.

"Let's go eat. Eleanor should have *our* mash ready by now. A man feeds his horse first, himself second."

As they crossed the yard, she noticed the fog was thicker. Arms and legs of it crept into the cobbled square between buildings. She shivered, glad when the house door swung open.

"Becky, come right on in!" said Charlie's wife, standing there in a red apron. "Charlie thinks more of his horses than his guests, I'm afraid, to keep you out in the damp," she added with a smile. Her face was pretty, a healthy pink framed by tarnished silver hair. Charlie replied with a big horsey grin, patting Becky on the shoulder as they entered the warm kitchen.

Supper was spread on a red-checkered cloth: pea soup with ham steaming in earthenware, slabs of both orange and white cheddar cheese, Eleanor's homemade bread thick with butter, and apples. They sat down immediately. Tea with milk followed the soup, and oatmeal cookies. (Becky couldn't get used to calling these "biscuits," as the English did.) Charlie remained silent while his big jaws worked over the food. Now and then he nodded to his guests to refill their plates or cups.

At last, when all were satisfied and well into their second cups of tea, he shoved his dishes to one side, planted his elbows on the table and rested his chin in his hands. He sat motionless a long time while Eleanor asked Becky about this and that.

"Now then—" he cleared his throat, looking earnestly at her father and her—"I need both your brains for a while. But first, help yourselves to some more tea." He pushed the pot toward them. "I really should have written . . ." He paused a moment and began again: "To be plain, there've been some peculiar things happen down here since I last saw you."

"Oh?" her father replied, reaching for his pipe and winking at Becky. On the way down he'd warned her about Charlie's habit of weaving mysteries out of a few odd, but not inexplicable facts. "Charlie," he'd said, "does not mind stretching the truth in the interest of a good story."

The big face glowed, warming to its subject, ignoring the note of disbelief in her father's voice: "You know that the Queen's Forest stretches for miles in back of us here—mostly pine with a few oak and other trees. Well, Findlay, the ranger who lives three farms down, asked me the other day if I was missing any horses. Seems he found evidence of horses loose in the forest, near the center."

"Is that right!" her father exclaimed, with faint enthusiasm. From the way Charlie smiled, she could see that her father's resistance was a joke between them.

Eleanor rose to clear away the dishes. Becky offered to help, but she motioned her back: "You can help me later." She smiled, yet cast a worried glance at Charlie. The dishes rattled as she carried them to the sink.

"Yes, a great trampling of hoofs in the pine needles—some droppings and such. I told him my horses never run loose." Charlie leaned forward. His eyes narrowed and his voice grew husky. "Hang me for a horse thief, but none of them was *shod*!" He pushed himself back, waiting for the surprise to register.

"So?" her father resisted, unimpressed. "Maybe there'd been a fox hunt, or some kids out pony trekking on unshod horses. You don't keep Rebecca shod, do you?"

"It isn't the season here for fox hunting," Charlie's voice rose with excitement, "and even if it were, *no one* is supposed to hunt in the forest. As for the other objection, Becky's unshod because she's retired, so to speak. Besides," his brows arched as his eyes grew larger, "I know every horse and pony for miles, and there aren't enough unshod ones to have done this." He struck the table with the flat of his hands, as if the case were closed.

"Well, what's your theory?" Her father gave in, letting the smoke out in a rush. Reluctantly, he propped his head in his hands and humorously rolled his eyes, but Becky could tell he was more interested than he let on.

"I dunno," Charlie paused, working the pause for

what it was worth and smiling mysteriously. "I confess I need help with this one. I suspect . . . there may be wild horses . . ."

"*Wild horses!*" her father exclaimed, jerking his head. "This isn't Wyoming." Charlie had been born and raised on a ranch in the American West.

"I know, I know." Charlie put up a hand. "Far-fetched! But so far, only the far-fetched helps. Findlay has been going out at night near the place, hoping to surprise whoever or whatever is making the tracks. He suggested we all take a look tomorrow—in the day-light."

He picked up an enormous calabash pipe and lit it with a flourish of matches, which he tossed one by one into the glowing grate. Becky's father said nothing, but winked again as Charlie stared into the coals, looking very much like a brooding Sherlock Holmes. Eleanor made soft puncturing sounds in her needlepoint.

"Ouch!" she said suddenly. "That's the second time I've pricked myself today." Charlie took the pipe from his mouth and looked at her as if about to say something. Then he put it back and turned resolutely to the fire.

The coals seethed and popped. Suddenly Charlie stood up and took something from the mantel. He turned to them with a look of subtle triumph. "And then there's always this!" He glanced nervously at Eleanor. "Found it myself and haven't told Findlay about it." It was a long thin shaft of wood, feathered on one end, with a bit of barbed bone on the other. He held it at arm's length, balancing the arrow between fingers and thumb.

"An arrow—what in the world?" Her father stood up and walked toward it, beginning to catch Charlie's enthusiasm. Becky got up too.

"Sent it to the British Museum. Got a letter back with it. Right here." He pulled from his shirtpocket a wrinkled scrap of paper and adjusted wire glasses on his nose: " 'Dear' . . . et cetera, et cetera. Here's the part: 'The arrow is definitely paleolithic—Old Stone Age— and exactly matches a design found in a recently exca-vated grave. Please tell us how you came by so exact a model of our find. Our tests of the arrowhead show it is made from the horn of no known animal.' It is signed by Sir Wolsley Piddlecott, himself."

"Not the great archaeologist!"

"The very one."

"But how—?" Her father had gone over com-pletely to Charlie's side, and Charlie looked secretly pleased.

"I found it sticking in a tree near the center of the forest." He ruffled the yellow feathers. "Model indeed! The markings show it was carved by a flint knife. Who'd bother to make a *model* that way? This is an original."

"Put it back up, Charlie." Eleanor's face was white.

"Excuse me, Dear," he bowed. "I forget— Eleanor doesn't like the thing," he continued in an undertone. "Gives her the creeps." He set it back in the shadows.

Then he turned and stretched, yawning. "We'll all take a look around tomorrow and you can judge for yourselves." He opened a door and whistled, adding, "Anyone for a stroll before turning in?" Two red shadows shot by the fire as twin Irish setters bounded to his feet and sat looking up expectantly. "Becky, meet Riff and Raff," he said, with a mock bow. The dogs looked at her eagerly, their long pink tongues laughing.

Out in the woods fog hugged the ground, which fell away behind the farm. From the valley below, the fog rose in weird shapes under a moon swelling toward the full. Pine needles underfoot smelled sweet, as the arc of Charlie's electric torch swung back and forth across the path. Riff and Raff bounded silently around them or paused and earnestly sniffed at trees.

"About four miles south of here," Charlie pointed the torch downhill, "stands a clump of oaks much older than these pines. At their center grows one at least 300 years old. That's where the hoofprints appear—out of nowhere, it seems. I could show you tonight, if it weren't so far." Fog swirled through the bright beam.

Suddenly Riff stopped, one paw in the air, tail straight out. A faint whinny traveled down the breeze behind them. Becky shivered inside the navy pea jacket Eleanor had lent her and stepped closer to Charlie.

"Hmmm," Charlie looked up at the blurred moon. "I wonder what disturbed Rebecca?" For some reason Becky felt relieved the whinny had not come from the depths of the woods. "The oaks grow in the center of a prehistoric earth-ring famous for years before they planted these pines," Charlie continued. "Now, hardly anyone visits it. We will—tomorrow."

"Is it one of those places where Druids worshipped?" Becky asked. She'd read in her book stories of pre-Christian Britain—of sacred holly and oak trees, and of human sacrifices burnt in wicker baskets.

"Perhaps," Charlie allowed, "but they think now the ring reaches further back than the Druids."

They turned around. Emerging from the trees they heard far off in the forest a second whinny, followed by a loud thump from the stable wall close by. Riff and Raff froze, growling.

"Rebecca's feeling her oats," Charlie said lightly, but his face looked thoughtful in the flare from a match as he lit his pipe. "Let's go to bed. Tomorrow's another day." They scraped mud from their boots and left them by the kitchen door.

The small, whitewashed room boasted little more than a bed, a chest of drawers, and an outdated calendar picturing a young boy half-hidden behind a log in a forest. He stood listening as sunlight streamed through the branches. He wore no shirt, and there was something wrong with his ears—they were too long.

The bushy eyebrows arched.

"Where have I seen him before?" Becky wondered sleepily, her shirt over her head. The wainscoting ticked. She wondered if the ticking in the wall was mice. Several horse journals lay beside the lamp, mostly uninteresting accounts of feeding and training horses. After looking at one or two, she threw them down. A number of horse nuts lay in a little dish on the night table. She wondered why they were there, then turned out the light and lay looking at the single window, which opened on the paddock behind the barns and stable. It was her favorite kind of window—made of small diamond panes and hinged to swing inward. The panes shone a dim gray, much like the chapel window where Lady Jane kept watch her last night in the Tower . . .

Suddenly a shadow moved across it and with a loud bang leaped into the room. Too surprised to cry out, Becky fumbled for the light. A large white head thrust across the sill. "Oh, it's you!" she laughed, as Rebecca bobbed and nickered softly. Apparently Dikkon wasn't the only horse who could open a stable door. "I can't *imagine* what *you* want!" She put her feet to the chill floor, clutched three horse nuts, and stepped over to the window. Rebecca's rough lips took one at a time. She crunched thoughtfully, then sniffed Becky's pajamas, looking for more.

"Stop that! It tickles," she said, trying to shove the big head out the window. It was no use. Finally she retreated to the bed. When she saw she'd get no more, the mare shook her head, snorted, and loped to the other side of the paddock. There she lifted up her nose and whinnied.

"Wonder what the old girl's up to?" Charlie's voice drifted in from another window. "Strange. The dogs are keyed up as well." Then she heard a window slam and his voice fade.

After sitting a minute in the dark, Becky tucked her feet under the flannel sheets, snug against the hot water bottle. It made her feel very sleepy. She closed her eyes and was snatched up by one of those jumbled dreams that catch you just as you're falling asleep:

"Tick, tick, tick," said the mice in the wall, and then a large mouse, who looked like Charlie, stepped out of the calendar swinging a gold light and said, "Did you hear it? Did you hear it?" Becky nodded her detached head up and down and whinnied. "I think it was an axe . . . an axe . . . an axe." Then darkness folded over her like a blanket.

Outside, the moon climbed higher as fog crawled away from the barns. A white horse stood by the fence, motionless except for an occasional twitch of her tail.

The Eye of the Fog

Inside the quiet house, Becky drifted back from the depths of sleep to those shallows which catch the light of dreams:

She wandered among trees larger than she'd ever seen. Leaves swam and flickered far above. Behind her a voice whispered, "Go until you find the way. Listen for the singing. Mind that you do not stop singing." Then the trees changed into horses and a white one trotted up and nibbled at her neck. It nibbled and nibbled and she couldn't push it away.

She woke to find her pillow on the floor and her head hanging over the bedside. A white radiance shone in the window and she got up to see what caused it. Except for one or two pockets, the farmyard fog had cleared. Yet, over the valley, a westering half-moon lit up an ocean of fog. Wraith-like arms rose from it, beckoning to the moon. The scene was breathtaking. She didn't notice her feet grow cold.

A pocket of fog stirred. Rebecca ambled across the paddock to the open window. She offered her the last horse nut, but the mare shoved it away and stood sideways against the house. As Becky moved to close the window, Rebecca whinnied in protest.

"Silly old horse!" Becky laughed. The big head turned and caught the edge of her pajama top, tugging gently. A thrill moved down her ribs. "Rebecca, I do believe you want me to ride you," she murmured. The head nodded and nickered.

The idea was preposterous—or would be, in daylight or under a different moon. As if in a dream, she slipped into levis, shirt, and sweater, tied her sneakers, and climbed over the sill onto the broad white back. It was damp, but warm.

The horse's big bones shifted under her. She was glad it was just a ride about the paddock. "I'll get off in a moment," she whispered in one ear, patting the warm neck.

Rebecca, used to giving such rides, plodded slowly around the ring. Then, just as Becky decided to get off, she turned with a snort and cantered in a straight line toward the gate. "Stop!" the girl cried in a loud whisper. The horse paid no attention, but at the last moment veered and galloped halfway round the ring again, her rider hanging on for dear life. Once again she turned and bolted toward the gate. By this time Becky was too scared to cry out. A few yards from it the old horse rose miraculously in the air, clearing the top rail by inches. She landed in full stride, galloping down the slope toward the black wall of trees.

"Stop!" Becky pled with her, no longer in a whisper. "Please stop!" Her words vanished in the air rushing by. The fog parted as they sped, and like a dark hand the forest opened to receive them. Rebecca continued headlong downhill. At the bottom, she slowed to a trot. But this made things even worse. Becky bounced awkwardly on the old bones. It took all her strength just to hold on, and the insides of her legs were soon chafed sore. At last, Rebecca shifted to a loping canter. Becky found this pace bearable and clung weakly to the mare's neck.

Dark pines loomed up and swept by, the moon a bauble fluttering in their branches. Its dim light lit a ribbon of trail. As she looked ahead, she received a second shock. This was the same trail she and Charlie had walked on earlier, the one leading to the center of the forest! Wildly she looked back toward the farm. But trees had long cut off any sight of it.

After what seemed hours, Rebecca slowed to a walk. The mare breathed heavily, but gave no sign of stopping. Again Becky pled with her and tried bare-handed to turn her head. Trees stared darkly down, moisture dripping from their needles, as the moon flickered between them. Now and again she ducked as a branch swept low, drenching her with dew. She considered jumping off but was afraid to return without Rebecca. What would she tell Charlie? She comforted herself with the hope that once the old mare tired, she'd turn back of her own free will.

It was silent in that eerie fog, except for the soft *thump thump* of hoofs. The trees lined up on both sides,

mutely welcoming her among them. She shivered. Each
tree passed was one closer to that mysterious ring Charlie had mentioned. "Why must you go in *this* direction?" she asked, angry and frustrated and kicking the
horse with her heels. But Rebecca ignored her, nodding
in rhythm with her hoofs—*thump, thump, thump*.

In the weeks since they'd left America, Becky
hadn't been the least homesick. Now, clinging to the
back of a horse gone wild in the night, she felt for the
first time thousands of miles from all she loved. Her
mother, her blue bedroom, Hrothgar's golden coat and
warm tongue stood like figures in a dream against a
brilliant Massachusetts sky. The white clapboards of
her house, yellow in September sun, the heady smell of
Concord grapes, even the mica chips glittering in her
front sidewalk, rose up before her. She saw her sister
Gwen throw a green apple over the roof and the gold
leaves of the big maple shake as it fell through them.

Again and again she asked herself why she had
ever gotten on the horse. She imagined her mother saying, "You're too impulsive, Becky!" Like the time she
couldn't wait for Gwen to finish developing the film and
had opened the darkroom door, spoiling all the nega-
tives. But that was different: she'd been eager to see
those pictures. Had she really been eager to mount the
horse? It was more as if the horse, fog, and moonlight
had arranged it. All had appeared so beautiful and
dreamlike—so weird. That was the word. She'd felt the
same that day in the Tower chapel. Now that feeling
had landed her on a runaway horse!

It seemed hours had passed, and Becky was thoroughly cold and miserable, when the trail made a sharp bend to the left. Along her right lay a deep ditch. Behind the ditch, an embankment rose ten to twelve feet. Large beeches grew on it. The path curved along the ditch for a few minutes, then took another turn through a cut in the bank. Both bank and cut looked man-made. Once through it the ground flattened again and the path wound among oak trees. All at once it dawned on her—a ring of earth! This was the ring Charlie had mentioned.

A prickly feeling climbed down her neck and settled in the middle of her back. So this was the center of the forest! She grasped Rebecca's mane to steady herself. "Hold on," she told herself aloud. But her voice sounded shaky and small. At that moment, the trees parted and Rebecca came to a stop in a clearing.

She couldn't see trees on the far side—nothing but fog and the dim moon above. Rebecca, head up, ears alert, stood as if waiting for something. Soon Becky felt a breeze, and the fog parted a few yards in front. She caught her breath. Not twenty yards ahead was the largest oak she'd ever seen, as thick as Rebecca was long. Its branches, festooned with ivy, bore mountains of leaves into the air. The topmost branches disappeared in mist.

Transfixed by the tree, she didn't notice a figure slip from its shadow. The moon brightened and then she saw him, standing absolutely motionless as if stamped from bronze. There, tail falling in a graceful arc, ears pointed and clustered with curls, chest bare in the blue light, stood a man with the body of a horse.

He stared straight at her, his mouth open, holding a long stick in one hand. Then the fog closed in again. Rebecca whinnied, and a shrill whinny answered her from the direction of the tree. Becky stared at the thick fog, not wanting to believe her eyes, hoping to wake up in her warm bed. But the soreness in her legs was as real as Rebecca's bumpy back. Had she seen what she thought, or was it a trick of the fog? It looked like a centaur, of all things!

She'd read about centaurs in the book on ancient mysteries. They were a myth, the book said: half-human and half-horse, wild, unruly, and terrible in battle. One of them, Chiron, was famous for wisdom. He had taught archery, music, and the art of healing to Achilles and other heroes. The heroes were also mythical—or so the book said. She put her arms around Rebecca's neck, closed her eyes, and begged her one more time to go home.

But Rebecca shook her mane and with a snort trotted ahead. Again came the shrill whinny, now from behind and to the right, followed by a muffled shout, a thud, and a short scream. This time the prickly terror wouldn't let go. Why had she ever climbed aboard this . . . this *night*mare? Rebecca galloped faster. Through gaps in the fog Becky caught glimpses of something—or *things*—running parallel to them. Here and there appeared a hoof, a tail, an arm. Once she glimpsed a human face, hair streaming straight behind it. The face was screwed up in pain and blue in the moonlight.

Then the sounds broke fully upon her. Horrible sounds: confused shouts, thuds, cracks, and groans; the clash of metal on metal, and a constant drum of hoofs. Points of light flashed in the fog, and fire gleamed from a blood-red torso. Now and then things whizzed overhead. Once, she heard a long, tapering moan. Then the sounds ceased.

She was riding toward a brightness. "The moon!" she cried. "It's clearing!" and took hope that her ghostly companions would disappear with the fog. But as it brightened, the fog thickened, until she could hear and see nothing, not even the horse's neck under her hand. The damp soaked her shirt. Breathing grew difficult, and she thought she must choke, when at last a dim outline of trees appeared. In a moment, they burst from the fog into a circle of oaks swathed with ivy.

"Alone at last!" she exclaimed, heaving a sigh of relief. But even as she did, Rebecca stopped and turned expectantly toward the fog. "Go on!" Becky yelled, kicking her ribs, "Go—" But her voice failed as from the fog thundered a splendid and terrifying sight.

It was the centaur, bearing down on her at full gallop. Ten yards from her he stopped, hair in his eyes and face glittering with sweat. In half a second he'd bent his long stick. Becky stared, fascinated. His chest heaved and dark fluid dripped from one shoulder as he aimed an arrow straight at her.

Rebecca screamed, rearing up on her hind legs. Becky slid backwards and felt something grab her from behind. A high-pitched voice yelled, "Don't shoot!" Then she swam in darkness.

"Why, it's a girl!" a voice was saying as Becky came to. "I don't think she has anything to do with the Rock Movers." Opening her eyes, she saw a full moon, framed by three heads, directly above her. The heads were connected to bare torsos, which in turn were joined to the enormous horse legs only inches from her head. For a moment the picture swam again.

"I don't know," a deep voice continued. "Those fiends will use any kind of trick. But she's a prisoner now, so we can't kill her. There's been enough killing tonight." Becky blinked and turned her head. Two of the hoofs had white socks—blue in the moonlight.

"Look—she's coming to." She recognized the high-pitched voice that had earlier yelled, "Don't shoot!" Two of the figures—one female—stooped and helped her up. On her feet, she found herself staring into eyes dark under shaggy brows. The centaur scowled:

"Who are you and where are you from?" His voice was stern. His head bore a mass of curls, some plastered by sweat against his forehead. The dark fluid from his shoulder trickled down one side. It was blood. "Tell me quickly!" His eyes flashed angrily. He held an arrow loosely nocked in his bow.

"I—I'm Becky, and that horse—" she burst out, looking wildly about for Rebecca—"brought me here from Canters, near Dunsfold." Rebecca stood a few yards behind her, calmly pulling up mouthfuls of grass. She looked up and snorted. As Becky turned back to the centaur, she caught a glimpse of a human form twisted in the grass. It lay very still.

The centaur stared at her for a moment, as if he didn't believe her. Then, before he could speak again, the ground shook and the oak circle flooded with centaurs galloping out of the fog. Tails, hoofs, and bodies flashed everywhere. The air rang with glad greetings and cries of dismay. The newcomers gleamed with sweat and lather; blood dripped from untended wounds. One was limping. Light coats and dark, shaggy and short, milled about in the clear moonlight. Human torsos, joined to horse at the pelvis, swept up to muscular chests and broad shoulders. The females' hair fell to the waist. The males' curly hair clustered about their ears. Each was armed with a bow and bore across the back a thick quiver of arrows. On faces frighteningly large, eyebrows curved up toward pointed ears. One by one they noticed her and stared.

They gathered around her, stamping feet, swishing tails, and talking excitedly about Rock Movers, ambushes, and something called the Eye of the Fog. Then a bearded one pushed his way among them and raised his bow in a gesture for silence. The first centaur walked over to him and whispered something in his ear.

The leader frowned and replied, "I don't know. It's not for us to decide." He stared thoughtfully at Becky for a good minute. In the silence came the wail of a distant horn, thin and quavering. Small hairs rose on her neck. The sound woke the leader from his revery. He looked behind him and said in a quiet but commanding tone, "The fiends collect their dead and wounded, but they will soon be after us. There's no time to lose. We will question the prisoner later."

Without a word the centaurs lined up under the oaks. Two lifted Becky onto Rebecca in the middle of the line. At a sign from the leader, the column filed into the forest.

The events of the last few minutes had happened so fast, Becky'd had no chance to think until now. As they moved under the trees, her situation became painfully clear: She was alone among dangerous monsters who had almost killed her. They were at war with another group. Whatever these others were, they sounded even worse. She hoped that it all would turn out to be only a bad dream. But real ivy creepers stung her cheeks as she ducked the branches.

They no longer followed a path. The forest, instead of pines in neat rows, was a wilderness of oak trees larger than she'd ever imagined. The moon was lost in the leaves, and she could barely see the hindquarters of the centaur in front. Then for a moment, the moon appeared in a clear space above a dead tree, and with a shock she realized it was a *full* moon—not the half moon she'd left shining over Canters.

Silver Garth

All this was too much for her. She sank into a daze
through which the events of the next twenty-four hours
passed like a dream. Certain pictures stood out in her
mind, however, though she was never sure she got them
in the right order. In the first it was dark and the sound
of rushing water grew louder and louder. The hindquarters in front disappeared under a black surface. Rebecca
followed, and Becky was suddenly wet and cold and
fighting to stay on her back. Then the big horse struggled for a foothold in the bank opposite. Cold air struck
like a knife through her dripping clothes.

In another picture they stopped on a hill overlooking a valley. Far below, points of fire wound toward
them. The leader spoke: "As I feared, the Rock Movers
follow us with torches. Let's hope the river stops
them." She had looked for lights from Canters, from
anywhere—a road, a farmhouse. But there were no
other lights.

Next she remembered a sky rosy with dawn. Centaurs drank from a clear pool, scooping up water in their hands. Others tended to wounds. She was famished. The bearded one gave her dry food from a pouch. The mix tasted like oats, raisins, apples, and honey. Ever afterwards she linked that sweet taste with the first hour of dawn. She got down off Rebecca and drank from her hands.

Then there came a second hilltop. From it she saw nothing but a vast carpet of trees. Here and there mist hung in a line to mark a river or stream. The distance showed one or two small clearings, very far apart. Now the hills rose sharply, much rockier than any she'd expected to see in England. Once a centaur cried out and pointed to a distant ledge. A large catlike creature, fangs curling below the jaw, froze a moment against the sky, then vanished.

Last, it was afternoon. They galloped through rolling grasslands divided by flowering wild hedges and giant beeches and elms. They galloped openly, coats flashing shades of red in the dying sunlight. Not even the wounded seemed tired; nor did Rebecca. Dazed and weary, Becky wondered at the flowers and green leaves flourishing so late in November.

About sunset they reached the edge of a hidden valley and climbed down into thick beech trees. At the bottom they found a path winding between smooth boles. Soon lights glimmered among the trunks and a minute later they halted by a cluster of barnlike structures. The walls were of upright logs and the roofs thatched with leaves. Centaurs moved in and out the large doors.

These dropped what they were doing and ran to greet the new arrivals with loud cries. The air buzzed with talk of Rock Movers and battle. Groans of anguish rang out as some discovered the wounds of friends. Others called for torches.

Becky was too tired to feel curious. She felt nothing but a desire to lie down. Inviting yellow lights shone through windows. She dismounted and started to walk toward them. At that the new centaurs noticed her. They pressed around so close she was in danger of being trampled, until the bearded one came to her aid.

"Back!" he said. "You shall hear from the prisoner soon enough. Now let her pass."

As they parted, a white-haired centaur stepped stiffly from a bright doorway. He carried an oaken staff wound about with holly, and in the torchlight his face shone wrinkled and sunburnt as an old apple. He stared at Becky a moment and then struck the earth with his staff.

"What have you done, Cavallos?" He turned gruffly toward the bearded centaur. "You know it is a crime deserving death to bring one of the divided kind within a day's ride of the village!"

"I know that, Father," Cavallos replied, putting a hand on his shoulder, "but there was good reason." He whispered in the old centaur's ear.

The latter cast a keen look at Becky and muttered, "We shall see. We shall see." He then motioned for her to follow him through the door into a longhouse.

Becky was too tired to notice much else. Someone gave her steaming broth, which she couldn't finish. Soon a kindly face laid her down on a pile of pine boughs. The same rubbed a fragrant salve on her chapped legs and covered her with a blanket. Overhead, firelight flickered on green boughs woven in the roof. As she fell asleep, she heard strings struck and a voice take up a chant.

She was wakened by a rustling noise. Opening one eye, she saw green lights move on the ceiling. It was a moment before she recalled where she was and recognized sunlight playing among the green boughs of the roof. At each end of the longhouse, bright squares of daylight shone. She was nearly alone. A long table and raised platform occupied one end of it. At the other, two female centaurs, one white and the other dappled gray, bent over a pot from which bubbled a delicious smell.

When they saw she was up, they called to her. She walked over and one silently gave her a wooden bowl and spoon. In it was something hot and steaming that looked like oatmeal, but wasn't. It tasted even better than it smelled, warming her all the way down. The first bite reminded her how hungry she was, and she sat down in the light from a window to finish it.

With her stomach full, her predicament struck her head on. Fainting at the centaur's arrow, clinging to Rebecca in the river, swaying dangerously back and forth on the endless gallop—these hadn't allowed her time to feel what she felt, now that she was out of immediate danger. She was miserable—more alone than ever before in her life. She dropped the empty spoon and bowl and stared at the dark unfriendly walls. Even the sunlight coming in the window seemed strange and awful. A lump swelled in her throat as she thought how worried her father must be, and how sad her mother and sisters would be, at the news. Suddenly both cheeks were wet and she made a choking sound.

For some minutes she felt worse than words can say. She was just thinking of her bed and Hrothgar coming to look for her every morning—finding it empty forever and ever—when, *wham!* a noise followed by a high-pitched laugh forced her to look up. There was a scuffle at the door. In a cloud of dust a shape sprang through it shouting something and came to rest, forelegs spread, in front of her.

"Excuse me!" a girl's voice apologized as Becky stood up. "Hippo was chasing me." Inches from hers grinned a face so darkly tanned the freckles were nearly invisible. Soot smudged one cheek. The face was framed by tow-colored hair falling to the waist. The rest of the coat glowed a golden palomino, except for two white socks on the forefeet.

"Who?" Becky asked, quickly wiping her cheeks.

"Hippocenos—Hippo for short. He's after me because I beat him at our shoot." The grin spread wider under green eyes. "By the way, I'm Lala—that's short for Lalagé. I already know you're Becky. And I'm going to be your special friend." She held out both hands.

There was something familiar in the voice. "Why,

you're the one who cried, 'Don't shoot!' " Becky exclaimed, seizing the hands. Her voice shook. She added, with just a trace of the sulks, "I suppose I should thank you for saving my life."

The smile faded; the green eyes regarded her side-long through pale gold hair. "You don't have to, though I'm glad he didn't shoot. He wouldn't have missed. That was Flimnos, our best archer." Her eyebrows drew together and she looked very serious. "It must be hard, being taken prisoner."

Becky didn't know what to say to this, and so she asked, "Why did you—did *they*—kidnap me?"

"Because the Rock Movers ambushed us and some thought you were one. *I* could tell you weren't, even in the moonlight. You don't look at all like one. Or," she paused, a puzzled look on her face, "if you *are* one, you're sure different from the others." Becky guessed this was meant as a compliment, and smiled. "I'll tell you a secret," Lala brightened. "I wasn't sup-posed to be on that scouting party, but I ran after and tracked them for two days. When I showed up in camp one night, my Uncle Cal—that's short for Cavallos—got very angry. But he said it was too late to send me back, so I might as well come along." She looked extremely pleased with herself.

Becky didn't know what to make of this girl cen-taur who could be happy and sad and talk a blue streak all at once. She asked, "What do they plan to do with me?"

Lala frowned. "I'm not sure." Then she smiled.

"But I'm going to do everything possible to save your life!"

At the news her life was still in danger, Becky said "Oh," and sat down. Yet Lala looked so crestfallen, she laughed in spite of herself. The two female centaurs were watching them closely. No doubt they were meant as guards. Lowering her voice, she asked, "Where are we?"

With a smack, a green apple struck Lala on the hindquarters—followed by a crow of triumph. One of the women centaurs ran to the window scolding. The girl scooped up the apple and was out the door in seconds. ". . . back soon!" The words trailed after her. Through the window Becky watched her gallop into the trees after a stocky boy-centaur. In the distance rang two high-pitched, whinnying laughs. Her loneliness returned.

She leaned on the sun-drenched sill, burying her head in her arms. Then something silky and warm rubbed against her neck. She looked up.

"It's you. Oh, Rebecca!" she cried, hiding her face in the long mane. She hadn't forgiven the mare for carrying her off from Canters, but forgot that as she hugged her. She noticed how much younger the horse looked in daylight. Her coat was glossy and her eye bright. "You're a bad horse—do you know that?" she said, half-scoldingly. Rebecca nickered and gently nipped her arm.

"Why, I believe you *understand!*" Becky exclaimed. The horse snorted and nodded, walked a few steps off and pulled up a swatch of grass with a toss of her mane. Behind her, in the village square, a centaur was treading a large wooden wheel. Becky watched with interest, forgetting her woes. A spout next to it gushed water, which a second villager caught in a jar. A large hay wagon crossed in front of them, pulled by a pair. The wheels, painted red, gold, and blue, stood taller than a man. At the far edge of the village a group huddled around one bending a bow. The bow straightened and hands clapped the bowman on the back.

A gong sounding behind her made her jump. Her female guards started talking excitedly among themselves. Everyone outside dropped what he was doing and headed for the longhouse. Becky followed them into the hall. At the far end behind the platform she saw the gong. A boy struck it a second time.

"High Council . . . High Council!" a sonorous voice intoned through the door. Behind the herald walked Cavallos, and behind him, carrying his staff of office, came the white-haired centaur of the night before. As the village lined up along the sides, the old one climbed stiffly onto a platform at the far end. When everyone was in place, he knocked his staff three times on the boards. The hall grew still. Shafts of hot afternoon sun poked through the green roof, spotting the earthen floor.

The old one struck the boards a second time. In a voice like an organ pipe, he boomed out, "Send the prisoner to us!" For a moment Becky wondered who the prisoner was. Then, from behind, a hand squeezed her elbow.

"Good luck!" Lala whispered. "His name is Senecos." Becky felt dwarfed walking between the two ranks of centaurs. Their dark eyes followed her, glinting in the light from a tripod that burnt before the leader.

"Sit there," Senecos commanded her, pointing to a small stool. "Now, let us have silence."

Becky wondered what he meant, since the hall was already quiet. Senecos folded his arms and closed his eyes, as did all the others. The silence lasted three or four minutes. Becky never forgot the sight of those hundreds of half-human, half-equine bodies absolutely motionless, glistening like bronze in the fitful light from the tripod. For a moment it seemed as if they were frozen in a painting. For one instant she thought she heard a strain of wild music, far off. Then, just as she shook her head to see if she really heard anything at all, it ceased. A second later they opened their eyes.

Senecos regarded her from under bushy white brows. His face was stern, but his voice held a trace of sadness. "Daughter of man, we question you now according to the law of our people. Tell me, why was one so young riding with the Rock Movers?"

Becky had the worst desire to fidget. Her voice sounded thin and small as she answered, "I wasn't. I don't even know who the Rock Movers are."

At that the old centaur's face stiffened. "You don't know who the Rock Movers are? Where, then, are you from?"

"I'm from Massachusetts," she replied nervously, then added, "But I was visiting Canters at Godalming in Surrey when that horse out there ran away with me and then . . . here I am, among you."

Senecos looked at her sharply. *"Canters? Surrey?* I've never heard of those villages." He took a step forward and shook his staff. "Do not lie! I warn you, your life hangs in the balance. Never has a two-legged one seen the village of Silver Garth before and lived to tell of it. It is the law."

There was an angry murmur of agreement behind her.

Just then, Cavallos stepped forward and put up his hand. "Hear me, Father. I think I can discover whether she is telling the truth or not."

"Proceed then," Senecos nodded toward him.

"Becky," Cavallos said, in a not unfriendly tone, "in that place you speak of, what kind of forest did you ride through?"

"The Queen's Forest, sir." At this, there was a second murmur from the crowd.

"What does this, er, 'Queen's Forest,' as you call it, look like? What kind of trees grow there?"

"Pine trees—spruce, fir, whatever. All I know is they're evergreen."

Cavallos' eyebrows arched higher. There was a note of excitement in his voice. "And how are the trees *arranged?*"

"Arranged?" Becky responded. "I'm not sure I know what you mean, but they are planted in rows."

Senecos cried out impatiently, "What has this got to do with the truth, Cavallos?"

Cavallos gave a great sigh of relief and smiled. "Father, do you recall when we last met in council, you commanded us—at the request of the First Ones—to travel through the Eye of the Fog to another time and to wait there for whatever happened?"

"Yes, of course I remember. What of it?"

"Even though we didn't know why the First Ones commanded this, we obeyed. Two dozen of us went to the Eldest of the Oaks and passed through the Eye of the Fog into a time many ages hence, into a time when the great oak forest will have vanished, except for a ring of trees and a descendant of the Great Tree itself. In that age" (here he made a face) "the whole forest is nothing but pine trees *planted in rows*!" At this news a groan passed over the audience.

"Many nights we revisited that time and waited. Some of us saw bright lights on the horizon. Others could hear the sound of metal grinding against metal, with many tiny explosions." Here he imitated the sound of a motor car. "But no one came near and nothing happened. The air was not clean and the stars shone very dim." He shook his head. "It is a bad time!" Another sigh moved over the centaurs like a wave over the sea. "Every dawn we would return to our own time."

"On the last night, the fog was thicker than usual. As we returned through it to our own time, we were ambushed by Rock Movers. We had been careless. Apparently they saw tracks we left around the Great Oak and were waiting for us. Fortunately, the fog was thick. We fought them in it, unhorsed many, and escaped. Many of them will not fight again. Flimnos nearly put an arrow through this girl, whom he discovered in the fog. He took her prisoner. I thought then she was a most unusual member of a Rock Mover war party. I began to suspect she came with us from the other time."

Every head turned toward Becky, but she no longer saw them. *Another time!* The shock of this phrase went right through her. The feeling of being lost in space was nothing compared to the feeling of being lost in time. If the centaur was right, Charlie, Canters, and her father and mother were somewhere thousands of years in the future, were *not at all* in the present time! It was as if they had never been. And, of course, they never *had* been, not in this time. Gradually the terror rose to her head. Black spots swam before her eyes; her ears rang. She fought to stay conscious.

At a great distance, she heard Senecos say gently, "Tell us, child, of your own time."

Part of her wanted to cry out but was too numb. She sat there pressing her palms into her eyes, fighting the panic. At last she found her voice, and numbly, slowly, began her story. Her tongue was thick. She had to repeat many things before the centaurs understood. Her listeners shook their heads in pity or disgust as she talked about the metal bird that roared through the sky to England and the cart that ran without horses.

At last, Senecos knocked a third time. "It is enough," he said. "We are convinced the girl is from the far future. Now we must decide her fate.''

"Senecos!'' a sharp voice interrupted him. A flushed and scowling centaur stepped forward. It was the one who had nearly shot her. "This two-legged creature may not be a Rock Mover,'' he began, "but she is clearly their descendant. In her time they are even worse than in ours, making this world unlivable with their metal horses and birds. I say that we hold by the law!'' He clenched and unclenched his fists.

"No, Flimnos.'' Senecos glanced shrewdly at him. "This girl has done nothing to harm us. Try to forget what the Rock Movers did to your family. She cannot help that she wandered by accident into the Eye of the Fog—if it *was* by accident.

"Fear not!'' He looked at Becky kindly. "For the moment you are safe. In the morning, we shall send a messenger to the First Ones in the West. The First Ones shall say what is to be done with you. The messenger should return in a week. Meanwhile, you and your horse are guests of Silver Garth.''

At this there was applause and ear-splitting whinnying on all sides. Senecos held up his hand. "First, however, it is only courteous that we answer our guest's questions, even as she has answered ours.''

Still in a daze, Becky asked the question uppermost in her mind: "Where—and when—are we?''

Senecos replied gently: "We are still in the same land you say will be called *Ang-Land* or *Brit-An*, though not for thousands of years yet. This land has many names—all of them true, if not all the same. For us, it is

A-Kentauros, Land of the Centaurs. You say that in later ages A-Kentauros will be an island, but now it is still connected to the mother land by a narrow neck that our forefathers crossed ages ago. Yet we know you speak truth, for with each century this neck of land grows smaller." He paused and looked at her.

Becky asked, "But how do you—did *I*—travel through time?"

"That is a mystery. None knows how it happens except the First Ones. At times of great need, they have given us power to travel through future time in order to escape danger. Many are the ages we have visited. We have such a need right now. Our people are rapidly becoming extinct because of the hatred and greed of the Rock Movers. Yet we know from our travels in time that the future no longer holds a place for us.

"Yours is a very unfriendly time in which all trees are planted by men and in which there is no room for centaurs and their kind to run free. Yes, I'm afraid only the First Ones know the purpose of our most recent journey through the Eye of the Fog."

Becky felt ashamed and wanted to defend her own time but couldn't think of anything to say. So she asked, "Who are the First Ones?" For some reason the name made her uncomfortable.

Senecos stared thoughtfully at her for a moment, cleared his throat, and said, "We centaurs came to Brit-An, as you call it, hundreds of years ago, driven north and west with other harmless peoples by the ancestors of the Rock Movers. We came west with fauns and satyrs, the wood and water peoples, and the remnant of the First Ones. They led us here. Very few of the First Ones still live, however, and their lore, which protected us for many ages from the Rock Movers, has been largely lost. The few who survive live in secret places in the hills to the west.

"But it is getting late." He looked at the others, spreading his arms. "Let us feast in our guest's honor and tell her more about us when she has eaten. Meanwhile, in the morning a messenger shall depart bearing news of her arrival to the First Ones. They shall decide her fate." He knocked with his staff three times and the council was over.

The Thing That Is Not ·

The longhouse was a hive of activity, with centaurs running in and out, starting cook fires, and setting the table. Lala took Becky's arm and steered her outside. She mounted Rebecca and the two cantered west of the village in the late afternoon light.

"Don't mind what Flimnos said." Lala smiled, as they stopped and turned around. "Now that he's had his say, he'll decide he likes you and that it was *he* who saved your life."

"I won't forget who did!" Becky flushed.

Sunlight glowed on the roofs as they ambled toward the village. The longhouse or great hall faced west. In front of it stood a well, the pump-wheel she'd noticed earlier, and an open square. To the north and south of the single street clustered smaller houses and pavilions.

Behind the village soared the tall beech woods through which they'd come. Supper fires winked invitingly in most of the houses. The sound of the gong drifted over the meadow and they galloped back to the hall.

As the sun dropped like a red cinder, stews, soups, and platters of roots made their way around the great trestle table. Seated upon Rebecca, Becky had the place of honor, to the right of Senecos. Fresh hay and oats had been provided for the horse, who nibbled them daintily, on her best behavior. Along with an endless variety of foods, bowls of a frothy brown beverage were passed. The centaurs were all in high spirits. Much joking and laughter flew about her head. Oil-soaked rushes burned in brackets on the wall behind them.

"You and Rebecca are a *two*-headed centaur," Lala teased, holding a morsel of bread out to the mare. But she snorted and turned back to her oats, blowing the bread into Lala's soup. Their end of the table erupted in laughter, and the elders had to stop a bread-pellet war that broke out among the boys.

"Rebecca's a bit of a windbag," Becky explained, patting her neck.

"Feeling her oats is all," a centaur with bright red hair and a broad grin replied, after draining a bowl at one swallow. He winked at her. Rebecca rolled an eye at him and twitched an ear.

During the meal Becky learned that Silver Garth housed most of the last tribe of centaurs. It was called "Silver Garth" because of the rye (among other grains) it was famous for. The rest of the tribe lived in two hamlets, Rootholm and Applehame, a few miles to the east and north, where the soil was better for fruits and vegetables. These few hundred were all that had survived the long wars with the Rock Movers. So far the three villages had remained hidden from the enemy.

After the dishes had been cleared, bowls were filled again with the bubbling drink, and a glistening harp was placed on one end of the table. A centaur with blond beard and curls struck it forcefully, and the table grew quiet.

"Is he going to sing?" Becky whispered, leaning toward Lala.

Lala nodded. "That is Greenleaf the Bard. He sings, as well as tells stories in verse."

At that, in a high chanting voice accompanied by strums on the harp, Greenleaf began the story of Kalendos and the Thing That Is Not, frequently glancing at Becky.

"Good! He's telling you about the First Ones, as Senecos promised," Lala whispered.

The poem was very beautiful and had in it all sorts of things that Becky forgot. But what she did remember she put down much later—in prose. Here is what she recalled:

"Once, in the morning of the world, all the peoples lived at peace with each other and with creatures of the wild. The First Ones ruled the peoples, speaking the languages of all. In those days the sun had not been thrown off his course, and the moon shone every night, neither waxing nor waning.

"The whole earth was a garden. Tree did not strive

with tree, even in the darkest forest. There were no summer and winter, as we know them. Summer covered most of the earth. North of summer was a belt of spring, then a land of fall, and finally, near the top of the world, a region of eternal snows. The talking creatures visited them all.''

For some minutes, a faint noise had filled the air. Soon Becky realized the centaurs were humming a low chorus to Greenleaf's words. It rose and fell with the pitch of his voice, then divided into many strands weaving themselves around his words. The murmuring chorus never detracted from the tale as his voice rose in a chant and fell to a whisper.

His tone grew stern as his hand struck a harsh chord. ''Then desire of the Thing That Is Not fell upon Kalendos, cleverest of the First Ones. For days he brooded among the trees and would not go forth to walk in the fields, or swim, or sing with his friends. All who spoke with him were confused, and said that Kalendos' mind had darkened with desire for the Thing That Is Not. The Thing That Is Not, Kalendos said, was on the tallest mountain in the West, and he would climb after it.

''In vain did his bride Floria remind him of music, stars, and the waters of the earth—pleasures easy to find and open to all. He would not listen to her but lay in their bower of leaves, his eyes closed, dreaming of the Thing That Is Not. The Thing That Is Not, Kalendos said, could not be described. Even he had only a dim idea of it.

"One day he disappeared from among the First Ones. He walked and ran for many days until he climbed the slopes of Sun's Home, tallest mountain in the West. But when he had panted up the last few feet, he could not find the Thing That Is Not. He sat there three nights, and on the third night a dark figure appeared to him in a dream, holding a blazing stone. 'Behold the Thing That Is Not,' the dark one said. Kalendos longed for it with all his being and his hand closed over it. When in the morning he woke, he opened his fist. Some say he found nothing. Others say he found a stone black as coal but hard as diamond, and as highly polished. When he looked into it he saw himself reflected infinitely. It was like a black hole down which his eyes might fall forever.

"Whatever it was, the stone turned his mind. He faced the sun and cursed it. As he descended the mountain, his mind wild and darkened, clouds rained a rain such as had never been. Fire fell from heaven, igniting a forest near the First People."

He paused. The humming voices rose in a long wail toward a climactic silence. During the silence Becky looked around at the faces, upon which shone an ancient and unassuaged grief. Tears streamed down cheeks.

Softly, Greenleaf continued: "In some later stories men said that fire was the Thing That Is Not and gave glory to Kalendos for stealing it from heaven. But they were mistaken, for Kalendos did not care for the fire but wandered raving into the East.

"One day, many years later, descendants of Kalendos came out of the East. They were a proud people who used fire to melt the earth's bones and to work metal. Because of this art, they pretended they were better than others. A quarrel arose and one of the First Ones was slain.

"In their guilt, the man-slayers fell to the worship of darkness, trying to appease it with the blood of creatures, including blood of men and women. Eventually, their descendants became the Rock Movers, so named because they move huge stones hundreds of miles to build temples to the stars. By these they measure the days, the seasons, and the years. By these they try to fix the future and make themselves secure against the evil that dwells in their own hearts.

"Still, the First People waxed more beautiful even as they dwindled. They ruled the creatures and spoke in their wisdom of other worlds whose beauty was so great that the smallest sight of it reduced one to tears of longing—beauty that blazed like the stars and upon which the Shadow had not fallen. Such a world is Alpha Centauri, Home of the Centaur, where oceans break on translucent cliffs ten thousand feet high, and winged horses nest in the lords of trees, and purple grasses run forever under a violet moon."

At this his voice fell to a whisper and ceased. There was a long pause—long as the silence earlier that afternoon.

Finally, someone else struck the harp and sang a comic song. More drink was poured amid much chatter.

Then Greenleaf began more tales. There were stories of battles with the Rock Movers—some that were won and some that were lost; stories of lovers and poets who spied on the fauns at their midnight dances; and, finally, the story of one who rode the great swan Halabath over the edge of the world. Becky grew sleepy, and still the voice went on. She must have dozed, for the next thing she knew Lala was gently shaking her. Without a word, she rose and stumbled to her bed.

The morning broke clear and glorious as Becky and Lala stepped out of the longhouse. A pink flush covered the eastern sky. Rebecca snorted and pranced up sideways, her coat wet with dew. As Becky mounted, she heard a shout from the far end of the village. A figure galloped away from a group raising their hands in farewell.

"That's Nikos on his way to the First Ones." Lala's eyes followed the diminishing figure. "I wish we could go with him." Becky said nothing. She did not share the wish.

Lala tossed her head. "Anyway, let's run!" She started off south across a broad field, her heels scattering dew brilliant in the rising sun. Rebecca lifted her head, snorted, and soon overtook her. Becky, who'd been too frightened or tired to enjoy earlier rides, found the speed and the fresh morning air exhilarating.

"Where are we going?" she called out.

"You'll see," Lala said turning, her grin accented by one dimple. Across the field, fat willows shone pinkish green in the rising sun. Behind these glittered a river. Lala splashed in up to her knees, stooped to drink, and then plunged into a pool in the shadow of an ancient willow.

"Come on in," she half-gargled, but Becky held back. Rebecca sloshed in up to the fetlocks, swished her tail, and buried her mouth in the water. In a moment Lala was out on the grassy bank, shaking water off her hide, rolling in the grass, and waving all four feet in the air. She looked so much like a large dog, Becky couldn't help but laugh.

"I do that every morning," Lala said, knocking one ear to get the water out. "You should try it."

"I will—later." The air smelled so fresh and springlike that the feeling of a great weight pressing down on her had very nearly disappeared. Food, rest, and the friendliness of Lala made it seem more like a holiday than a captivity. Anyway, she knew there was nothing she could do about her situation until the messenger returned. Very sensibly, she resolved not to worry until she had to.

They galloped over a second field, this one of clover, and into a little wood which opened out in its center. A green carpet of leaves shedding a few last blossoms couldn't hide the red fruit winking underneath.

"Strawberries!" Becky exclaimed.

"The first ones of the year," Lala replied, handing her a leather pouch. They picked and ate until they were full. Then they lay down in the shade and talked. Lala's mother and father had been killed during a Rock Mover raid, and she'd been raised mainly by her Uncle Cavallos and his wife, Biana. With great satisfaction she told how she'd tracked her uncle's scouting party after they left Silver Garth and then one night showed up in camp.

"Uncle Cal got over it when I proved I wasn't a pest. Anyway, I can shoot nearly as well as Flimnos." She picked up her bow and shot a pine cone off the top of a nearby tree. A squirrel came out and scolded them. They laughed.

At noon they rode back to the river, swam, and lay in the sun. Lala kept the berries cool by putting wet leaves over them in the shade. Becky shared her own past with Lala, who was not as unhappy as her elders about the inventions of Becky's world. "I'd like to fly," she said, closing her eyes and putting out her arms. "They say there are horses that do so on Alpha Centauri."

In midafternoon they rode back to the village and joined a party going to the beech woods to dig for medicinal roots. She met Hippocenos, a plump boy with light brown hair and freckles, who kept teasing Lala. Also, Georgos, who was thin and very dark, with black hair. Georgos brought along a leather ball stuffed with straw. After a while Hippo threw it at a convenient backside and the herb party broke up into tagball. Then they divided into teams for hoofball, a kind of soccer or polo. Because Rebecca had no idea of how to kick the ball, Georgos cut Becky a long stick to use as a mallet. Everyone on both sides cheered whenever she managed a hit.

They arrived home after dark and were chided by the mothers as they seated themselves around glowing coals. For supper there was venison and small round cakes of bread—hard to chew, but savory, and, of course, the cool, sweet strawberries. Becky felt sunburnt and deliciously tired. She fell asleep by the fire as the others were singing a round. It was about beechnuts, chestnuts, and hazelnuts growing green under the white stars of midsummer.

The next day was hot, and Becky, after joining Lala for a bath in the river, followed her to the cool shade of a pavilion—a house almost as large as the longhouse but with no walls. There, stretched out on looms, were colorful blankets and tapestries in all stages of completion. A tall female with chestnut coat and dark blonde hair asked Becky if she would like to see the work. She had a wonderful smile.

Lala introduced her. "This is my Aunt Biana." Biana put her arm around Becky's shoulder as she showed them about. First she explained the weaving of intricate patterns through the movement of warp, woof, and shuttle. Then she showed her the tapestries. The largest had scenes of a battle on one panel, a great white stag on another, and, on a third, stars between which lines were drawn in the shape of a centaur. It was yet incomplete.

"That is the constellation of the Centaur," Biana explained. "Alas, it's not visible in our heavens." Just then a needle came poking through from the other side and they heard a grumble. Biana took it and guided it back. Smiling, she whispered that Sartos, the master tapestry-maker to whom she was apprenticed, needed her assistance. The girls tiptoed out.

Hippo, puffing and clutching his bow, nearly tripped over them as they emerged blinking at the bright sun. "Flimnos . . . an archery shoot!" he gasped and was off in a cloud of dust. At the end of the street they saw Rebecca trotting behind a crowd of young archers. She followed about after any excitement, and Becky believed the mare actually enjoyed watching the centaur games. They soon caught up with her.

An average centaur archer could hit an apple at fifty paces, and an expert, at a hundred. Becky watched as Flimnos split five yellow apples, one after the other, at a hundred paces—two arrows in the air at once.

After the applause died down, he set up a contest among his pupils, which included nearly all the young of the village. It took the whole afternoon and finished with a duel between Lala and Georgos. The latter was ahead 4 to 2, when Lala won the match by sinking three in the bull's-eye. Flimnos handed her a gold-fledged arrow—her trophy to carry until the next match. Then he turned to Becky.

"Now you try it," he said, his voice considerably softer than it had been two days before. He selected a bow and arrows and patiently showed her how to use them. The other centaurs watched quietly. After two shots went wild, she shot one that stuck soundly in the edge of the straw target. The whole company cheered and Rebecca whinnied twice, at which everyone laughed. The horse seemed to grow more coltish by the day. Her coat was glossy and her back had less of a sway to it. She spent hours in the pavilion with Biana, who talked to her while weaving. The horse twitched her ears and nodded from time to time in response.

The third morning, Lala left Becky to visit Scopas the Seer, a very old centaur, blind and partly crippled, who lived west of the village on top of a hill. Lala was preparing for her Dreaming, as it was called, and needed his counsel. During the Dreaming, a young centaur would come to know her hidden name, a name she kept secret for the rest of her life.

"You mean, you never tell *anyone* this name?" Becky asked, marveling.

"No, it is between you and the Shaper," Lala replied shyly. Becky resisted asking her who the Shaper was. The name left a curious prickly feeling at the back of her neck.

At noon Lala returned at a gallop, her face flushed, eyes flashing with delight. It seemed that morning an older cousin and her fiancé had presented themselves before Scopas with a circle woven from the hairs of both their tails, a symbol that their lives would be woven together forever. After a feast that night, they would leave to spend a month near the warm springs of Naphturi, where flowers bloomed the year round. Excitement in the village was doubled at the noon meal when Biana announced her sister Rhuana had given birth that morning. All were invited to the Standing.

Late that afternoon Lala and she accompanied Biana and others to the last house on the right. Inside they found Rhuana looking tired and half the size she'd seemed the day before. Lying next to her was a red, plump baby on a long foal's body. He was only a few hours old, with light down on his head, and his coat the rare palomino. In a few minutes he tried to get up, mixing up his legs and tripping over them. Within a half hour, he made it to all four, to the cheers of the on-lookers. His mother blushed with pride. A garland of daisies was placed around her neck.

Afterwards, Biana explained that the use of four good feet was absolutely essential to the centaur's life. Eyeing her thoughtfully, Lala asked Becky if it weren't frightening, balancing along on only two: "Every time you take a step you fall forward until the other foot catches you." Becky smiled but experienced a small thrill of wonder at the thought.

One morning, after she'd been there a week, Becky noticed none went to the fields or swept up after breakfast. Instead, without a word they formed a pro-cession out of the village. As she joined it, Lala caught her eye and made a sign to be quiet. The procession wound up a hill to the southwest and into a glen of small oaks halfway to its top. The glen was about fifty yards in diameter and walled on the west side by a cliff twenty feet high.

On top of this stood a very old centaur, his face wrinkled and his white eyebrows drooping over deep-set eyes. She guessed it was Scopas the Seer. In the silence he began to hum, and soon a swelling of sound rose from all throats but hers and joined as streams join together in a river. The sounds were all different but harmonized. Becky understood no words, only a melody or theme that moved from within the circle toward the outside and back again. All the centaurs stood very still, their heads alone swaying, their faces lifted to the sky. The music was at once the most beautiful and sorrowful she'd ever heard.

When it was over—minutes, maybe hours, later— she felt a great joy she couldn't explain. Everything, every leaf and blade of grass, seemed much stiller, much more *there* than it had been. Lights and colors and fragrances from the wood were more intense. Time moved slowly, more distinctly. The rest of the day, she and Lala picnicked far upriver by a waterfall. Neither said much, though both bathed in the clear falling water and swam in a green pool at its feet. Words would have taken away from the fullness of that sun-drenched day.

The Black Stag

On the morning following the quiet day, breakfast was interupted by a great shout to the west. Mouths full of food, Becky, Lala and others ran outside to find a centaur galloping toward them. It was Nikos the messenger. His black flanks covered with lather, his hair streaming, he hardly slowed as he pounded up the street. A crowd gathered to meet him by a stone horse-head known as the Listening Post. Nikos gasped as lather dripped from his sides. At last he wheezed out two words: "Rock Movers!" Everyone froze.

Between breaths he explained how, returning from the First Ones, he'd met a tribe of satyrs. "It was Flint-hoof and his family," he puffed. A few nodded. They had heard of Flinthoof. The satyrs were fleeing because a day's ride south and west they'd sighted a party of fifteen Rock Movers. Apparently a hunting party, the Rock Movers were headed southwest, away from Silver Garth. Yet no Rock Mover had been seen that far west before. So the satyrs had decided to move north into the wilderness of Hardros. The crowd broke into an anxious murmur.

Then a deep voice asked, "What did the First Ones say about the man-child?"

"I have their message and it's serious," Nikos frowned. "She must . . ." But catching sight of Becky, he broke off. "I'll tell all at the council." At that he broke away and trotted toward the longhouse.

Biana looked at Becky with a worried expression, but Lala lit up: "A council—good! I'll strike the gong." She was off like a bolt, but the villagers were already gathering in the longhouse before it sounded. Becky felt sick to her stomach. Over the last week the beauty of Silver Garth, the wonders of life among the centaurs, and especially her new friends, had very nearly put the First Ones out of mind.

Senecos stood on the platform, his face grim. Below him, to the left, waited Cavallos. On his right panted Nikos, thin and long-legged, an ideal runner. Even Rebecca was there, head thrust in the window, ears forward. Lala stroked her nose as Nikos repeated his news about the Rock Mover hunting party.

A cry of dismay passed through the house. "Silence, silence!" In vain Senecos struck the boards with his staff. It was minutes before he restored order. "Tell us what the First Ones commanded regarding the girl Becky."

Nikos hesitated, glancing at her. "She must go to them as soon as possible."

Heads turned her way as he began his account. On the morning of the fourth day, he had been met by the First Ones in their rocky-walled valley or canyon. Blindfolded, he was led a long way around to their hidden meeting place.

"The Cavern of Lights," he said, "lies behind a screen of falling water. The lights from the water play over the ceiling. In the wall opposite is a narrow window that looks upon the sea. From waterfall and wave many colors shimmer over the walls and the robes of the White Ones.

"My eyes had only a moment to adjust before Menos appeared. He is indeed as old as they say, if one counts wrinkles, but strong of limb and voice. He heard my story of our fruitless search through the Eye of the Fog and how we found this girl and her horse. Then his mouth lifted and his face glowed. He questioned me closely about the time she was from. Finally he said, 'It is urgent that you send her to us at once. She may be the one we are looking for. There is an old prophecy:

> *Trust the horse to know the rider*
> *And through the night and fog to guide her.*

However, not much time remains. Send her at once!' He waved his arm and I was blindfolded. As I was led out I heard him call after me, 'And she must come *alone.*' Three days later I met the satyrs."

The word *alone* ran in one long shiver down Becky's back. For a week she'd forgotten that she was alone in this strange time. Now she was to be alone again on a dangerous journey to creatures who sounded hardly human. For what could they want her so badly that they had summoned her out of the future? Lala came over and whispered enviously, "How I wish I could go too!" But these were the wrong words. Becky turned her face to the wall.

As if at a great distance, she heard someone cry out, "Tell us more news of the Rock Movers. What are we going to do about *them*?" Again, everyone talked at once—the older centaurs saying they should move to a place further west or north, the younger pointing out that by so doing they would lose the half-grown crops and miss the best of the midsummer hunting. Others wanted to pursue the Rock Mover party immediately, yet it was clear the thought of moving had been on everyone's mind for months.

"Silence! Silence!" Senecos finally quieted them down. "The First Ones have spoken: Becky will leave in the morning. Now that we know she is the one the First Ones require, we will delay any decision about the village until she returns. Or," he added ominously, "until ten days from now—if she doesn't return."

"One minute!" Cavallos stepped forward, his face red. "Surely we will not let this girl travel *alone!* Not on a dangerous road, with the chance of meeting Rock Movers!"

"It would be unwise to disobey the First Ones in this matter," Senecos said gravely.

"The last day—the day she enters their valley—she can go on alone," Cavallos persisted. "But we must escort her to the valley head."

Senecos thought for a long minute. "My heart misgives me on this matter, but I think you're right—with Flinthoof's news, it would be barbarous to send her on that road alone.''

The rest of that day was hard for her. Not even Lala could keep up her usual high spirits, though she would be part of the escort. She sensed Becky's heaviness. What's more, it clouded over and rained for the first time since she'd arrived, and supper was a silent affair.

That night in her sleep, Becky dreamed of water rushing, voices chanting, and an enormous shadow rising on the wall of a cave. She woke to find Scopas the Seer standing silently by the tripod, apparently deep in thought. She watched him.

Biana had told her that most centaurs left the village upon growing old. They went off into the western hills to prepare for the Great Change that follows this life. There they were instructed by the First Ones in the art of standing still—still as Scopas was now. Occasionally one like Scopas would return and live near the village to give counsel and to share his wisdom. Becky saw the seer take a pinch of something from a pouch and put it on the burning tripod. The whole house filled with a smell that reminded her both of leaves burning and the first thaw of spring. Somehow the smell comforted her.

She was wakened before the first light and moved in darkness to put her pack (ready the night before) over Rebecca's withers. The centaurs going with her shared a cold breakfast of oat cakes and milk. Then they gathered at the Listening Post for a final check of their gear and to say goodbye. Lala was there, holding a splendid bow and a green quiver filled with new arrows. Before Becky could admire them, Lala handed them to her.

"Flimnos made these for you in order to make up for his earlier gruffness. He wanted me to present them for him."

The gift overwhelmed her. The bow was tipped with horn as was each arrow. Her shooting was not up to so fine a weapon, and she knew she'd been done a great honor. She looked around for the Chief Archer. He avoided her gaze. As she was strapping the bow to Rebecca, Cavallos came up.

"I wonder if the First Ones will know what to make of you." He patted her affectionately. But the remark, though well-intended, didn't help her feelings. The First Ones might be very old, wise, and good, but that made them no more approachable. She wasn't at all sure what was meant by "good" in this ancient world. Her brooding was interrupted by Biana, who hugged both Lala and her.

"Be careful!" Biana said, embracing Cavallos. He looked gravely at her, then smiled. "No fear! It will be a holiday." At long last he turned from his wife and gave a command. The group lined up. Rebecca nearly threw her rider, attempting to be first in line behind Cavallos. Lala hurried up alongside and laughed at the mare.

Becky never forgot the fresh, cool morning they started. The whole eastern sky was touched with pink and the grass white with dew as the party wound quietly out of the sleeping village. For the first half-hour they noticed the signs of early morning—a rabbit scurrying to its hole, raising a mist and leaving dark tracks across the smooth grass; an owl rapidly flying west; the stirring and chirping of birds. Then the land ahead of them flushed pink. They stopped and turned to watch the red disc of the sun free itself from the horizon. Far to the west, Becky saw the gleaming pink tops of a line of mountains. Lala smiled and nodded toward them: "The western hills."

Cavallos was a good companion on such a trip. He pointed out every variety of flower, tree, or rock. The day passed in talk among the three. That night they camped in a wide meadow under a large willow. After the others were asleep Lala poked Becky and silently led her to a place out of earshot.

"Do you recall the shining world Greenleaf sang of?" she whispered.

"Of course," Becky whispered back. The grass was wet with dew and the trees cut crisp shadows against a sky powdered with more stars than she had ever seen.

"There it is—the Path to the Stars." Lala pointed toward the southern horizon, her arm black against the heavens. Following her finger, Becky made out four stars in a line. "That is the Arrow pointing the way to Alpha Centauri, second most brilliant of the fixed stars. Alas, we are too far north to see it."

"Have you ever?" Becky asked, deep in wonder.

"No. Long ago, before Senecos' great-great-grandfather, our tribe lived in a warm climate by a gentle sea. There we could watch the constellation of the Centaur and gaze up at our bright home in the skies. Then we were driven north, but the Arrow in the sky was here to point the way over the horizon to Alpha Centauri. It is our true home, though we were born in this one. It is a world where men have never gone the twisted way." Her voice grew dreamlike. "In that world there is no killing. One may live forever in forests where birds are as big as centaurs and trees rise higher than mountains. There one may walk along bright stones on the ocean floor among creatures who sing the tides to sleep."

Becky held her breath. Alpha Centauri, if it was the same she'd read about, was the star closest to the sun, and could very well have several planets spinning about it. Its neighbor star circled so close that with the naked eye the two appeared to be one. As she gazed heavenward, she saw the familiar Big Dipper and the Little, the North Star, and of course the Milky Way. How beautiful they were, and permanent. How many times had she gazed on the same heavens from the security of her own bed thousands of years in the future?

The second day they passed through a lightly wooded country with long grassy allées between rows of trees. The rolling fields and hedgerows, Cavallos explained, had once been planted by the First Ones, before their numbers dwindled and they retreated to the hills. In the afternoon heat he paused by a large rock. He and Becky were a good way ahead of the others, and he called her over, scratching at the moss on top. "I believe this is one of the Singing Stones set up by the First Ones," he said, as he exposed the carving of a hand. It pointed west. "If we were to dig down its whole length, we would find the stone at least fifteen feet tall. Several feet from the top are intricate holes through which the wind would whistle or hum. There are probably others around—likewise buried by the drifting years—for the First Ones would carve whole choirs of these stones for the wind to play on."

As Becky looked at the stone, she felt as she did in churches filled with statues of people who lived long ago. It was a pleasant feeling, with just a tinge of sadness and a longing for she knew not what. The trees whispered above her. Shafts of sunlight leaned against the stone, grass, and leaves, bathing all in a yellow light belonging to old paintings. The earth gave off a sleepy smell.

She looked up at Cavallos, who was pensive too, and said, "It's sad to think of those people living here so many years ago, looking at this stone just as we are."

"Sad?" asked Cavallos, his mouth bending in a grave smile. "Yes, it is sad, because of what some men have made of the world, because of hopes gone bad and joys that wandered from their true course. But we ought not to be sad for most of *these*. For as they grew older the light within them shone more brightly, until some went about veiled. As their first strength lessened and their hair silvered, they walked to the singing of the stones into the western mountains. See, the hand points west.''

He paused as the sun, shrunk to a ball, bathed all in a red light and edged down over the treetops. "Sad?" he murmured. "There is nothing sad about these. The sadness we feel is the shadow which haunts us because, if we choose, we can turn away from the light.''

Hoofs on the turf behind and a glad shout from Lala told them the others had caught up. It was time to make camp. They scattered to hunt the hedgerows for dry brush and logs—hard yew, oak, elm, and fragrant pine. They made a fire in one of the small groves where two hedgerows crossed. Soon red flames flashed merrily off bronze flanks and black eyes. An iron pot was strung over the fire, and a bed of pine boughs gathered for Becky. Savory herbs and roots simmered in the pot along with meat from their packs. Even in the semi-darkness, the centaurs found pungent and edible plants. "The dampness helps," Lala said, wrinkling her nose. "We can smell them out more easily at dusk and dawn." Becky sniffed, but smelled only the sweet wood smoke.

After Becky cleared her second plate, mopping up gravy with the solid, unleavened travel bread, she accepted a bowl of drink made from a special root. She never could describe the taste exactly. The names helped somewhat, she said, but not much. The darker sort was called leafblood, and the lighter kind, leaflight. You could taste trees in it, and roots, and secret underground places, and the edge of fall and the first promise of spring.

The trees around them glimmered and changed expression in the flickering flames. Again, the feeling of the afternoon stole upon her, together with a foreboding that increased the longer they were in that empty land. She wanted to know more about these strange people who had sent for her.

"Tell me, what are they like, the First Ones?"

"Well," Cavallos shifted to a more comfortable position, sitting before the fire like a big dog, "they are mostly old. It is many years since they had any children. As they passed into the mountains, they learned to stand still for great lengths of time, gazing into the light—the sun by day and the moon and stars by night—until time itself stood still, and all days, past, present, and future, rose before them—until, rooted in one place, they seemed to be in all places. Yet, they sometimes leave their simple caves to do the few things they must to live. Sometimes they pause to speak with newcomers, or talking beasts, or the rare Rock Mover who flees to them for refuge. Their words are never taken lightly; rather, each is treasured as a jewel set in silver.

"So they live quietly, until the light in their faces and limbs burns too strong for the body. Then they call to two of their brothers that the time for the Great Journey has come. As the three sit, facing west, singing music from before the beginning of time, the shining spirit passes on. The frail body, like a dry leaf in the fall or a cocoon the butterfly has abandoned, is placed on a raft of reeds and given to the waves. The waves carry it west where the bright smith of the sun beats them to copper." He paused and stretched. "That is all I know. You'll soon discover more yourself."

After all had drunk again, eyes shone about the fire and a harp was produced. Together the centaurs sang:

> *Star of summer, caught above*
> *In thickening leaves, where is my love?*
> *Over wave, under sea,*
> *Through solid stone, she lingers . . .*

The song continued; Becky soon discovered it was not the usual sort of love song. The "she" of the song turned out to be different from what the lover imagined. No matter in what form he sought her, she always appeared in another, unexpected shape. As a kind of refrain, the teasing words "Not this, not that," were repeated again and again. Afterwards, Lala told a tale about a bride who wove a house of mats—splendid with rainbow colors—for her bridegroom. But he was wild and shy and would never sleep in the house. Laughing, he would call to his bride to leave her splendid house of mats and join him galloping over the moonlit fields.

Throughout the tale she noticed Cavallos was not listening. He seemed preoccupied. As the last flames sank to embers, he posted himself and another as guards. It was the practice, he said, this far from home. As she closed her eyes on her pine couch, Becky caught a glimpse of him through the trees, standing motionless at the edge of the grove.

She woke dreaming of a waterfall: It was coming down on her face and she kept calling to Lala to turn it off. She opened her eyes under a light sprinkle, rolled over, and pulled the damp blanket over her head. It was still dark. When she next woke, the dawn was dull and gray about her. There was no fire, and she shivered. Everything glistened with wet. The band quickly broke camp and were soon trotting through the steady rain. She marveled how the centaurs took pleasure in raindrops trickling down their bare shoulders and steaming flanks. She herself stayed dry under a skin Cavallos had thoughtfully packed in his bag. Lala, however, kicked up her heels and frisked alongside the path, hair straggling down her back in dripping points.

The centaurs' mirth made a pleasant day out of a gray one. Still, outside their little circle of high spirits, the groves appeared somber in the rain—even sinister. Cavallos alone among the centaurs was quiet and studied each feature of the landscape. Her earlier foreboding grew on Becky, as the groves watched them pass.

They came to an avenue between rows of large beeches and paused as Cavallos studied the grassy way for tracks. But the rain had evenly pitted the soil and washed away all sign of passing man or beast. A mile or so further they came to a crossing of ways. Two beech-lined avenues stretched north and south, as well as east and west, as far as the eye could see. The silence of the ancient trees reduced all talk to whispers. In the center of the crossing was another of the sunken stones with a hand carved on top.

Cavallos cried out and ran toward it. Someone had placed a clod over the hand. The dirt had obviously been there awhile, since rain had streaked it down one side of the rock. The leader's face darkened: "It's recent—within the last week. Maybe as late as yesterday. Too bad the rain has washed away his tracks."

"Who could it be?" asked Lala.

"Almost anyone—a centaur from one of the other villages—one of Greyflank's people, perhaps. Or a First One on pilgrimage—though he would know better than to desecrate a sign. A faun, or satyr, or . . ." He paused.

"Or?" Becky asked.

"Let's not mention *that* unless we have to," he said, and turned back to the trail. They went on, Cavallos scouting in front and two others on the flanks. They discovered no further clues. About midafternoon the clouds broke and a wonderful sun warmed them to the bone. Even Cavallos relaxed.

That night they camped in a grove of ivy-covered oaks. The fire was smaller and Cavallos would not allow them to sing. In the middle of the night Becky woke from a dream of flutes. She was sure a flute had wakened her, yet all was silent. A sliver of moon glimmered between leaves. She turned over. As her eyes closed, she thought she glimpsed in a far-off clearing the silhouette of a child—a boy with the hairy shanks of a goat and holding a pipe to his mouth. When she opened them again, he had vanished. Only the moon shone. She went back to sleep and dreamt of the picture in the bedroom at Canters.

Toward dawn she woke a second time. A shaggy face floated inches from hers. She was too surprised to cry out. The face was small and bearded, with long pointed ears and hair down over the eyes. What shocked her most was its expression—one you might see on the face of a startled dog. But the eyes were human.

Before she had time to speak, he turned and, with the whisk of a small goatish tail, vanished into the bushes. She rubbed her eyes, wondering if she'd dreamed it all, when she heard in the distance a flurry of drumbeats. Then silence.

Lala stirred beside her. "A faun," her whisper came. "He was spying on the strange creature we brought with us!" Becky could just make out her smile. "We must tell Cavallos. Perhaps the faun put the dirt on the stone."

When the morning mist lifted, the sky was blue. Everything glittered and twinkled in the early sun. Cavallos was relieved by the girls' news. "Fauns are full of mischief," he said. "No doubt he put the clay on the stone." Then, halfway through breakfast, the guards ran into camp all excited. They'd found the fresh footprints of a large stag, leading away from the grove. In three minutes the centaurs had scattered their camp-fire and packed to go, some rearing up on hind legs in anticipation of a hunt—for centaurs the most exciting sport in the world.

Together they examined the tracks, which led off south. Cavallos looked troubled for a moment, then held up his hand.

"Tempting as it is to hunt so large a beast, we must hasten on our mission to the First Ones." There was a general murmur of disappointment. Flimnos spoke up.

"Such easy game crossing our path will help make up for any midsummer hunting we miss. If we limit our hunt to the morning and travel at twice our usual pace this afternoon, we'll not be delayed."

Cavallos looked thoughtful for a moment and then smiled broadly. "In all my summers I've never hunted so large a beast. So be it! We'll spend the morning in the chase." The others cheered him loudly. Hunting was in the centaurs' blood, though they never killed except when they needed meat. Even Rebecca pricked up her ears, bared her teeth, and whinnied, much to the amusement of the others. As a young filly she had often run to the hounds.

They started off at a lope across an empty meadow, working their way steadily south, pausing only to examine the ground for tracks. Despite the sunshine, the early woods were silent. For some reason, Becky's uneasiness returned. She was about to mention this to Lala, when one of the party hallooed. She glanced down an alley of trees and saw something glossy and black leap into dark shadow.

At a bound they were off, the air sweeping back her hair. The sound of hoofs, of everyone galloping together, was marvelous. She never forgot the sight of Lala, face flushed, yellow hair blown back gleaming in the sun. Rebecca pulled in front of the crowd as Becky held tightly to her mane. Gradually Cavallos overtook her on the left. Soon these two were far in front. At the end of the natural alley, the path took a bend to the right, down a narrow ravine. Rebecca's pace barely slowed and Becky took a couple of rough bounces. Cavallos was now two lengths in front. Far ahead, where the ravine opened out, she glimpsed antlers flashing in sun. Cavallos lifted a horn to his lips and blew a high, sweet note.

Becky never had such a ride before! Her horse sped recklessly over the ground as if she had wings. The ravine opened onto a wide meadow lined on the far side by willows. Water glittered under these and in a minute she and Cavallos reined in at a riverbank. The stag was just climbing up the other side. He was a magnificent beast of many years, his head higher than Cavallos'—all black, except for his antlers and a brown patch under the chin. He shook himself and stared at them fearlessly. Cavallos put an arrow to his bow.

"Oh!" Becky cried out involuntarily at the sight of the beast's red eyes. The stag jumped and Cavallos fired at the same instant. The arrow nicked an antler and shattered against a willow tree. Before she could apologize, Cavallos had plunged into the river, Rebecca after him. The water was cold from the recent rains. They struggled up the opposite bank and sped toward a pine wood. Again Cavallos blew his horn. This time there was an answering note far behind them.

Once in the pines they saw the stag swerve off the main track up a ridge covered with gnarled oaks. They turned after it along a barely visible path. The oaks fell away on both sides. A third time Cavallos blew his horn, but this time they heard no answer. The ridge path ran for more than a mile, twisting and turning but clear enough for their hoofs. At the end it opened to a wide place surrounded by thick brush. A gap in the brush led steeply downhill. In the glade at the bottom loomed a large tree speckled with green apples. Apples dotted the ground under it. Rebecca clambered down the washed-out incline and came alongside Cavallos, who had stopped, looking down intently.

"Look at this," he said. There, by a smashed apple, was a fresh footprint—of a man, not a deer. She got down off Rebecca to look closely. Bending over, she suddenly felt a weight on her back and heard a soft plop. She tried to look up, but couldn't. Something snaky covered her. She tried to raise her hands but they were weighed down by thick ropes. She was caught in a net.

"Run!" Cavallos cried, rearing up next to her, trying to lift the net off both. But it was no use. Green figures stood on all sides. They had green faces— hideous monsters! She found herself screaming until a rough hand pressed rope into her mouth.

"Keep her quiet!" a voice came, cold and even.

The sound of a human voice was a shock like ice water in her face. She no longer tried to scream. As rough hands removed the net and held her pinned, Becky saw men dressed in green from head to foot. They had smeared green paste over their faces for camouflage. A dozen struggled to pin Cavallos under the net. They had him on his side, but his hoofs thrashed out. As one or two retreated from his flailing feet, he somehow managed to put the horn to his lips and blow one furious blast. But no answer came, except a curse, as a man leapt on top of him and put a knife to his throat: "Blow again and you'll choke on your own blood." Apparently this was the leader. He had long black hair and a thin face, corpselike under the green.

On Cavallos' back, holding his arms pinned and a knife to his throat, the leader ordered him to stand and move quickly into the trees, dragging the net. The others surrounded him with drawn bows. A large, dark-haired man forcibly carried Becky. His beard scratched her cheek and he smelled like garlic. Rebecca kicked out as a rope halter dropped over her head, but came peaceably when she saw Becky go. The green men hurried them a ways into the dense woods, sweeping away all tracks with branches. There they stopped.

The big man put Becky down but kept his hand tight on her mouth. All stood motionless. Becky listened hard for the sound of hoofs, praying the other centaurs would catch up. But she heard only wind in the leaves. At last, a thin smile twitched over the face of the leader. He turned around and barked an order. An emblem flashed from his chest: a black ram's horn circled by a ring of red stones.

"Rock Movers!" Becky exclaimed. The man with the curly black beard grunted and tied her hands with rawhide. The others guarded Cavallos, making crude jokes about centaurs, and cruelly poking him with arrows. Their leader, still on his back, ordered them to take up two logs—a long and a short one. They placed the shorter across Cavallos' shoulders and tied each hand around one end. The centaur staggered under the weight. The longer, thicker log they fastened to his rear leg by a chain.

"What are you doing to him?" Becky cried. Cavallos turned with a look of great sadness.

"Let the girl go," he said. At that, a guard lashed him across the face with a rope.

"Shut up, you talking horse!" he snarled. All but the leader seemed to find this funny. He dug his knees into Cavallos' flanks and said, in the same deadly tone, "Forward!" Blood ran down the centaur's cheek.

The curly-bearded man threw her on Rebecca's back and took the halter. Slowly, with difficulty, Cavallos dragged the log. The weight, Becky thought, must be incredible. Whenever the log caught against a root or stone, one of the guards lashed him before prying it free. Within a few minutes red welts crisscrossed his bare back.

· *Escape in the Dark* ·

All this time Becky listened with failing hope for the sound of the other centaurs. She gradually realized that even if they did discover their trail, they could do little against so many armed men. Within a quarter-hour the group arrived at an open glade, where others in green waited with the troop's horses.

A fat, red-haired man stood up and stretched. "Well, Flit, I see you snared a woodcock or two."

"No thanks to you," the thin-lipped leader sneered. "A buck and a useless wench!" He pointed at Becky. "A skinny stick. From the looks of her she belongs to those ghouls in the hills." (Becky gathered he meant the First Ones.) "And a nag that's seen better days."

At the insult Rebecca laid back her ears and kicked. The man holding her gave a harsh jerk on the halter.

"Well," the fat man grinned evilly and spat—three

front teeth were missing—"What they bring at auction will help pay us for this cursed venture. Let's go."

They formed a column along a path to the southeast. Some of the horses bore on their backs the skins of deer and heavy bags of salted meat hung on either side. The strong smell drew hordes of flies. Becky guessed this was the hunting party sighted by Flinthoof the Satyr.

They jogged along, her hands tied behind. She couldn't shoo the flies and they stung her nastily. The afternoon was hot, and sweat ran unchecked into her eyes. Yet she hardly noticed as she watched the clouds of flies fasten on Cavallos' bleeding back, his arms stretched along the rough beam he bore in silence. At the fat man's direction, the log he dragged was lightened by half its length so they could hurry. Yet the chain soon chewed raw the skin around his leg.

Between Becky and Cavallos rode Flit and the fat man. With relish the thin leader told his partner how he'd captured Cavallos and Becky. She strained to listen. Over thud of hoof and creak of harness, she heard enough to piece together the following story:

Under the guise of a hunting party, a hundred Rock Movers had ridden west from their capital city to find the hidden centaur villages. For weeks they'd had no success, except for a brief skirmish in the dark. (Becky figured this must be the ambush in the Eye of the Fog.) Then the Rock Movers had pushed further west. Since they knew there was coming and going between the centaurs and the First Ones, they planned to hide near the western hills and wait for a centaur to pass by, hoping to capture him and take him to their city.

After a day or two of hunting, they had swung north by night, sending scouts far ahead. Just yesterday a scout had spotted Cavallos and his band and rode south to tell the others. (Becky wondered if it was he who had defaced the stone!) She gathered he'd arrived among the Rock Movers at dawn. They rode north immediately and by midmorning heard horns coming toward them.

As chance would have it, the stag had fled down the very path they were riding up. Quickly, Flit set up an ambush. Some hid the horses, while the rest rigged up the net in the apple tree. It was a great stroke of luck and they had laughed as they worked, grinning at each other through the green paste. They planned to capture one centaur and shoot the others from ambush.

No sooner had they hidden when a black stag, foaming from the mouth, raced down the slope and through the glen. But they held their arrows, waiting for the centaurs. The rest of the story Becky knew only too well.

That afternoon was her worst yet. She felt so bad for Cavallos that she hardly noticed her own wrists, raw from the thongs that bound them, or her one eye swelling shut from the bites of horseflies. She saw the stripes on his back stop bleeding and cake with blood, only to open again under the lash. The sun expired in the west before they stopped and made camp.

The stained faces of her captors moved grotesquely about the fire. On horseback, Becky hadn't had much chance to look at them and was not reassured by what she now saw. Along with weariness and the soil of travel, these faces showed a restlessness, a discontent, not found on the centaur faces. The men were gruff and surly with each other. When someone tripped or did something clumsily, they laughed and called him degrading names—especially a large blond fellow named Tull. Tull did act half-witted at times, but his face was pleasanter than the others. His good humor irritated them, and one stuck out a foot that sent him sprawling into the fire. While the poor man beat out sparks on his clothes, the others howled, snickered, and guffawed. Tull retreated from the fire and drew a blanket around himself, blowing on burnt fingers.

After roasting strips of venison and greedily gorging themselves, the Rock Movers offered the scraps to their prisoners. Becky couldn't stand the smell of the half-raw flesh, however, and only drank a little water. She and Cavallos had been tied—tethered was more the word—to opposite sides of a large oak. By stretching her ropes as taut as possible, Becky could just see his head. Both logs had been removed and he lay on his side.

"Cavallos!" she whispered as loud as she dared. But the centaur's eyes remained closed; his face shone white and dead-looking. "He's fainted from the pain!" she said aloud.

Slowly the dark eyes opened and stared back through the dusk. "I'm sorry . . ." Cavallos whispered huskily. It was hard for Becky to catch his words. He closed his eyes again, paused, then opened them. "Sometimes my back causes red flashes and I have to close my eyes," he panted. "I'm sorry I got carried away and led you into this. It's all my fault. I should have kept the group together. And I was more foolish to blow—Shh!"

A dark shape loomed between the fire and themselves. Becky closed her eyes, pretending sleep. Footsteps crunched close, stopped a moment, then crunched away. For a second she smelled garlic and sour wine. When she opened her eyes, Cavallos had turned his back.

"Pssst!" she called. "What do they want with us?"

Slowly, with a painful grimace, Cavallos turned around. "I know what they want from *me*. They'll take me to their city and there by tor—by ways they have—they'll try to make me tell where the villages are."

"How will they *make* you?"

"They won't," Cavallos hissed through teeth clenched in pain. "But they'll try . . . anything."

A loud roar of laughter burst from around the fire. They heard a great thwack followed by a cry. A hulking figure broke from the circle and stomped past them into the trees where it stood making animal noises. It was Tull again—Becky recognized the thick, clumsy shape—and he was crying.

It was long before the two dared whisper again. "I know what they want from me," Cavallos repeated.

"What concerns me is what they want from *you*." He paused and forced a smile. "Of course, they don't know where you're from, or about your mission to the First Ones, which means they may guard you lightly. If so, you may have a good chance to escape. How you would find your way back to Silver Garth alone is another problem."

It was dark now. Becky clung to her last hope as she asked the question on her mind all afternoon: "Do you . . . do you think Lala and the others will track us?"

Cavallos sighed and for a moment said nothing. "They must have run right past where we turned up the ridge. Later, of course, they missed us. But whether they'll find our trail in time is anybody's guess. You, though, if you escape, might backtrack and find your way to the village. It would be dangerous—with wild beasts and worse about—but safer than staying with these fiends. And something else warns me that you must get to the First Ones soon. Now, how tight are your ropes?"

"Shut up you two," a voice barked from the fire. "You, Durn and Wart, tighten their ropes!" Two men came and tied Becky closer to the tree, throwing a rough blanket over her.

The fly-bites started to itch and she noticed the ache in her wrists was worse. Under that dark blanket all hope seemed gone. Leaving Silver Garth for the First Ones had been bad enough, but now, to be captured and perhaps killed or sold as a slave . . . The idea was too much for her. Weary with misery, she turned on her back, freeing her head from the blanket. The night sky shone clear. Through a gap in the leaves she saw four stars in a row, pointing over the horizon. Somehow the sight comforted her, and she drifted into an uneasy sleep.

The next day dawned cloudy and foggy. As it went on, Becky's hope that the centaurs had tracked them grew feebler. But the flies weren't as bad, and though Cavallos still had to carry one log and drag the other, the Rock Movers had lost interest in flogging him. Freed from immediate pain, Becky's thoughts again circled about her misery. Several times she had to shake off feelings of self-pity. Riding along she tried to focus instead on Cavallos' back, just ahead of her. It was crisscrossed with stripes, now crusted and dark. How they must hurt as they healed!

About noon the man leading Rebecca changed places with Tull. His speech revealed that the huge man was somewhat simple. But unlike the others, he would often look back at her, smile, and point out flowers, birds, and trees. He took a childlike pleasure in these things, and he laughed a high-pitched laugh when a jay swooped and startled Rebecca. "Afraid!" he said, pointing at the horse, and laughed again.

Then, with a worried frown, he looked up at Becky. "Are *you* afraid?" he asked.

"No," she said, though this wasn't strictly true. "Are you?"

"Sometimes," the big face replied, looking down

as its owner kicked a stone out of the path. "Soon we'll be home," he brightened. "There I'm not afraid." His face cleared and his eyes shone like two small skies.

With Tull's company, the rest of the day passed swiftly. By nightfall he had taken complete charge of Becky. The others gladly let him. He tied her so that the ropes wouldn't hurt and gave her an extra blanket—his own, it turned out. He cooked some tender pieces of venison and brought them over in a clean pan.

"Would you take some to my friend too?" Becky asked, chewing a savory bit. Tull's face fell.

"The others would beat me," he said.

"Do it secretly," she coaxed, "when they aren't looking. Pretend you're bringing them to me."

At this, Tull smiled a smile at once so crafty and gleeful that Becky could hardly keep from laughing. He brought a second pan of venison and crawled with it to the opposite side of the wild thorn, where Cavallos was tied. He returned, beside himself with joy.

"I'm glad you're here, Becky," he said. Then a cloud spread over his face. "But tomorrow we will be in the city, and they'll take you away." He wiped his eyes with his sleeve.

After Tull returned to the fire, Becky called to Cavallos. The centaur had overheard Tull's news. "Tonight's our last chance," he whispered. "See if you can work your hands free."

Fortunately, Tull had tied the thongs loosely and in a few minutes she worked one hand half-free. The knot proved too strong, however, and she looked around for something to cut the leather. One edge of the supper pan was jagged, making a crude saw. She rubbed the thong across this. For a long time nothing happened. She redoubled her effort. In half an hour the thong was worn through. Then she untied her feet. Bunching up her blankets to look as if she were still in them, she crept quietly around to Cavallos. He squeezed her hand as they paused a moment, listening. They heard nothing but one or two snores from around the campfire, now glowing embers. Far off an owl shrieked. Becky shivered.

Cavallos' hands proved hard to untie. After a while he told her to forget them and work on the rope tethering his hind feet. This she undid easily. As it dropped from her fingers, a shadow passed the fire. She leapt to her blankets and was under them when Tull came up.

"I heard an owl cry," he said. "I wanted to be sure you're all right."

"I'm all right," Becky said, trying to sound sleepy.

"Good. Go back to sleep." Tull shuffled toward the fire.

It was another half-hour before she dared creep to Cavallos again.

"Up on my back," he said, "but quietly." This she did, holding her breath. Trees were taking shape. Dawn was near and they must hurry.

Slowly, one step at a time, Cavallos backed away from the camp to where the horses were tied. It seemed to take forever. Once a twig snapped and they froze, but the noise failed to wake any of the sleepers. Silently they untied Rebecca and slipped away west. At least, Becky *assumed* it was west. With the coming dawn, fog rose and filled the hollows among the trees. She rode on Cavallos' back, working at the knots on his arms. Rebecca followed.

The woods were low and swampy; they had to pick their way along high ground. The fog rose to Cavallos' knees and soon they walked into a thick cloud of it. This forced them to go slow, feeling in front for branches. Nevertheless, Becky's face stung from whiplashing twigs. Once they fell into a bog up to the centaur's belly. Grasping Rebecca's tail, he climbed out, legs slimy with mud. With that, they stopped until the fog thinned.

"One thing's on our side," Cavallos broke the gloomy silence. "The Rock Movers can't track us in *this!*" At that moment they were pushing their way through pine branches that scratched and clawed. Just as they were ready to turn back, they found a path through the thicket. The path bent right and a little further on joined a wider, grassy track.

"I don't recognize this from yesterday," Cavallos observed. "Perhaps it's another trail. Anyway, moss on the bark shows west is that way." He started off at a trot. The fog above them thinned to blue sky and the first rays of sun felt good on their backs. Becky breathed easily for the first time since they'd escaped; a few more minutes and she'd have his hands untied. She was just beginning to wonder if they should stay on so well-marked a trail—for the others would surely pursue them—when they rounded a bend by a shaggy larch and almost collided with three horses. The first reared up and nearly threw its giant rider, whose face broke into a broad grin.

"Becky's back!" cried Tull—for it was he. Rebecca whinnied loudly and bolted west. But before the other two could join her, a cold voice behind them said, "Don't move, or I'll put an arrow through your heart!"

Rhadas the Magnificent

They froze. "Let the nag go," Flit continued in his level tone. "She's dog meat anyway."

Cavallos' shoulders slumped. "My second mistake!" he murmured to Becky. "We circled to the east in that fog and never should have risked this path." Rough hands removed her and a whip came down on his shoulders with a terrific crack.

To be caught again after having escaped was almost unbearable. Becky's hopes, so high a moment before, now struck bottom. And then, perhaps because they *were* at the bottom, they rose a little: if she and Cavallos had escaped once, they might escape again. Or Rebecca might find the centaurs and lead them in pursuit.

Two Rock Movers tied her hands and lifted her onto Tull's horse.

Tull looked up at her and she gasped. One eye was black and swollen shut. His nose bore a large purple bruise and his lip bled. A tooth was missing. The others had obviously blamed him for the escape. He smiled: "If you hadn't come back you wouldn't see the city and Tull would be sad." His smile widened. "But your hiding was very clever, very clever. Tull didn't know where you hid."

"It *was* a kind of game," Becky admitted to herself, then noticed a new trickle of blood down Cavallos' back. "A grim game!"

Past noon, the troop rode into marshy country. The trees grew short and scrubby, then thinned out. In the distance appeared a green wall. Soon the wall revealed itself as a mass of giant reeds, each topped by a plume. Through this the path cut, along a dyke or causeway. In a while the reeds opened out onto the largest river yet. It was at least 100 yards across, and every kind of waterbird flew above it or scurried into the reeds at their approach. The causeway ran along the river's edge for several miles, then turned inland and climbed to higher ground.

As they topped a knoll, the column halted. Becky held her breath. Before them, a mile distant, stretched the wall of the city. She saw now how the Rock Movers got their name: Enormous menhirs—large standing stones—were arranged in what must be a circle, though she could see only part of it. The largest of these stones rose over thirty feet. To complete the wall, smaller stones had been carefully laid between the larger. Along the top a parapet of logs—pointed and with loopholes—bristled with armed guards. The wall vaulted the river and continued on the far side.

Beyond the wall and higher than it, large stones made footings for a bridge in the middle of the city. She guessed some of these menhirs must be sixty or seventy feet long, including the part underwater. Topping the bridge was a row of houses. She could just make out people like ants moving along it.

Crossing the moat by a drawbridge, the troop passed through a main gate into the northern half of the city. Clumps of soldiers with peaked leather hoods stared down at them from both sides. They moved up a wide street toward what looked like a fortress. Crowds of people ran ahead of them and lined the street, craning their necks to get a view of the captured centaur.

Every size and age of face appeared along this street, with its thatched, peaked houses sometimes three stories high. The upper stories leaned out over the lower at perilous angles. Dirty, ragged children laughed at the centaur and called him names. Red faces of farmers and huntsmen stared without a sound. The haughty eyes of beautiful women glanced down from balconies and occasionally a man with gold rings in a glossy beard and a red sash over his shoulder paused to watch them pass. Most of the faces looked like those Becky had seen in other cities—hurried, anxious, and vaguely discontent.

The streets were noisy with the clop of hoofs, the creak of carts, the cries of vendors, and an oceanic murmur of voices. At each doorway a new smell jumped out—sometimes pleasant odors of food cooking, other times bad smells from crooked alleys that twisted away from the avenue. She noticed large birds circling above the bridge over little black knobs on top of the great stones.

At the gate of the fortresslike building, a guard disappeared inside. They heard three horns blow, each higher than the last, and an enormous wooden door with a ram carved on it swung open. They passed through and it shut with a clunk. They stood on green marble smooth as the surface of a lake. Dark red pillars rose on either side. Between them, bronze murals glowed fitfully in torchlight. A tiny strip of sky shone far above.

The sudden quiet was even more impressive than the hall; here the noise of the city was only a vague whisper. Becky squinted at the bronze plaque nearest her. It was a moment before she made out the shapes on it. A charging ram crushed underfoot a pipe of some sort. Fleeing from him was a faun. The look on the faun's face was both stupid and wicked. She wondered if some fauns looked like that, or whether the artist had just painted him that way.

A door opened at the far end and horns again sounded, this time louder than before. They moved forward. The soldiers marched stiffly, pausing at each step. "Eyes straight ahead!" Flit growled. From the corner of her eye, Becky glimpsed other bronze plaques. She couldn't make out all the figures, though she saw the ram several times. Taken together, they seemed to tell a story.

Light poured from the open door with a glittery

movement. They were entering a courtyard, partly open to the sky. Facing them, a seven-tiered fountain splashed in a pool of green marble filled with water lilies. Various songbirds hung in cages about the pool and their song blended with the murmur of the fountain. Through the falling water shone something gold.

They stopped inside the door, blinded for a moment by the brilliance. Then Flit, Cavallos, and she were led by a man in a red sash around the fountain toward the shining. Becky's knees felt weak until she saw how calm and dignified Cavallos looked. He made her feel calm in turn, and she lifted up her head.

The brilliant light came from an enormous ram's head set in the wall above a throne of red marble. The head was covered with gold leaf and glittered in the flames from two torches. On either side of the throne, in green robes with red sashes, stood three men staring straight ahead. On the throne itself sat a young man of about sixteen, with black curly hair falling in ringlets to his shoulders. He was dressed in a plain white robe and on his head rested a gold crown, from either side of which curled the familiar ram's horns. His face was thin and pale.

Over the throne hovered a man in a black robe. He was bald, but a black beard, curly as the other's hair, descended to the middle of his huge belly. He looked at least seven feet tall. Without warning he opened his mouth to an enormous O and boomed out:

"Rhadas the Magnificent, Master of Water, Earth, and Sky, Illustrious Prince of the Mines of Mordoon and the Quarries of Ack-Beth!'' At this Flit fell to the floor, as did the other soldiers. The young man on the throne stared impassively ahead. Becky glanced at Cavallos. The centaur stood unmoved, gazing steadily at the youth on the throne. The logs had been removed, but his hands were still tied.

Slowly, the youth raised one hand and motioned them forward. The large bearded man bent over and whispered in his ear. Rhadas whispered back, then looked them over thoughtfully. Becky sensed both curiosity and sadness behind his frozen expression.

The bearded one scowled and said, again in a loud voice, ''His Magnificence knows who you are and from where you come.'' He stared fiercely at Cavallos. ''In his wisdom he condemns you, foul sorcerer and unnatural creature, to die as a sacrifice to Phogros the Far-sighted.'' At the mention of Phogros, all in the room touched every finger on his right hand to his thumb, as if counting. Becky later learned it was a sign of respect to Phogros, the spirit worshipped by the Rock Movers. They believed it was Phogros who first taught man how to count, to divide things, and to control his days. But she hardly noticed that now.

''No!'' she cried out and ran to the centaur's side, throwing her arms around him.

''Silence!'' the fat mouthpiece shouted, and frowned at Becky.

''Daughter of man, your people who starve among the hills are half-crazed and thus let you fall into the clutches of this monster. In his sovereign wisdom and great mercy, his Worship has decided to release you from the evil bondage and magic of this sorcerer and let you dwell in the royal palace of Longdreth as a servant girl.''

Becky wanted to scream that he lied, and besides, she didn't belong to the First Ones, when she caught a warning glance from Cavallos. She bit her tongue. The guards brought forward heavy chains and shackled Cavallos' two arms and four legs, attaching weights to them all. The weary centaur did not resist. Then they flogged him stumbling from the room.

One of the guards held Becky back, picking up the struggling girl as the others whipped Cavallos. Hot tears blinded her for a moment and she screamed and bit and kicked, but it was no use. As she was carried from the room heartbroken, she caught a last glimpse of Rhadas. The ruler was staring at the floor.

The guard cursed Becky for a she-devil and crushed her to his knobby breastplate as they wound through windowless corridors lit by torches. After numerous flights of stone stairs, he knocked on a plain wooden door. A tall, hatchet-faced woman opened it.

''His Magnificence wants you to look after this she-devil,'' he said, throwing Becky down in a heap. ''By all the hairs of Phogros, she's flayed me like a faun!'' He rubbed his arms. Becky lay there silent, bruised and in shock.

''Nothing you don't deserve.'' The woman grinned at him nastily. She was missing a front tooth. She shoved Becky into the dim room and made her lie down on a couch. Then she shuffled back to the door and whispered to the guard.

Becky hardly cared where she was. A flickering lamp revealed a windowless garret room, one dirty gray wall slanting over her. Her couch was stuffed with straw and covered with the rank fur of a large animal. The woman leaned against the doorpost in a brown homespun robe tied at the middle by a green cord. Her hair fell stringy to her shoulders over sallow skin. One side of her lip drooped. Now and then she glanced at her new charge and laughed the same unpleasant laugh, poking the guard in the ribs. When she laughed, her lip drooped even more. The laugh rattled again and again as Becky sank into an exhausted, dream-filled slumber.

She walked past small red lights leading through endless corridors. Once all the lights fused together and she heard the sound of horns. The lights changed into a gold ram's head. The ram's head bellowed fiercely, but its eyes kept shifting, as if it were frightened. Then the face split open and a young girl with long curly hair stepped out. The girl tried to talk, but made no sound. Finally she wrote something on a rock and handed it to Becky. The words glowed like fire: "I must get out!" they read. Becky repeated them aloud several times.

"You'll get out soon enough if you do what you're told." Becky opened her eyes on the coarse face of the woman, who was shaking her. "You were talking in your sleep, wench. You'd better not wake me with that trick or you'll wish you hadn't! More than one around here can scratch." She held up a hand with long pointed nails and walked to the door.

"I'm going out now and will lock you in. Don't cause no trouble if you know what's good for you." She jangled a ring of keys threateningly. "Oh, yes, there's something for you to eat." She waved carelessly at a table with a clay bowl and mug, opened the door, and locked it behind her.

Becky examined the bowl. In it lay a strip of beef—tough but well-done—a hunk of dark bread and a lump of butter. She didn't feel at all hungry, but ate to keep up her strength. The food was plain but savory, and she was surprised how her appetite returned as she ate. Done, she turned to the cup. By the smell, it was warm beer or ale. She wrinkled up her nose and turned to a barrel of drinking water in the corner.

Hunger and thirst satisfied, she picked up the lamp and inspected the room for another way out. There was none. The door was thick and well made. She lay down and dozed again until the sound of the woman's key woke her. Her keeper, whose name was Brieda, was pleased to find the beer untouched. She drank it at one swallow, dragging her arm across her mouth when she finished. That, plus what she'd drunk when out of the room, made her talkative.

From her gossip, Becky learned she was in the back parts of the palace—"Not so nice as them apartments in front, though it's better than some," Brieda allowed. As a chambermaid, she felt she was a cut above the kitchen crew and the palace guards. "They're a rough bunch," she nodded. "Rude, full of insults, and will rob you blind. Keep away from 'em. Targ oughta burn the lot of 'em, but each owes something to Targ and is useful. He's got 'em on a string." She winked evilly and belched. Becky asked about Cavallos, but Brieda told her nothing.

"Don't worry about your friend. Forget him. You'll be better off without him." She grinned and flicked her tongue through the hole in her front teeth. Becky turned away. She found it hard to listen to Brieda's rambling talk but learned from it that Targ was the baldheaded man with the beard who'd spoken in the throne room; he seemed to be in control of everyone, including Rhadas, whom Brieda referred to as the boy-king. When Rhadas' father died, Targ had been chosen Protector to help the Prince rule until he came of age. Instead Targ had made himself tyrant. Becky also learned that Flit by capturing a centaur was back in favor with Targ after having been under a cloud for some nameless evil deed.

"If he'd come back empty-handed it'd been the quarries or the stake for Flit, I say, and good riddance!" Brieda spat on the floor. She mentioned the quarries of Ack-Beth and the Mines of Mordoon so often, Becky figured out they must be worked by a vast number of Targ's enemies. She learned too she was to become a serving girl. As soon as she'd shown herself "civilized," Brieda said, she was to be let out of her jail.

"And you'd better not act like them other young snips, who think they're too good for us," Brieda added, shaking a bony finger.

Over the next couple of days, Becky tried to learn

more about Cavallos from her guardian, especially when her tongue was loosened by drink. But Brieda either repeated stories she'd already told or responded with silence and an evil wink. "The less said, the better, Dearie, the less said, the better!" she clucked.

In the middle of one of these talks came a soft knock at the door. Brieda unlocked it and in stepped a girl about Becky's age, with hair so blonde it looked white.

"This is Neetha," Brieda said coldly. "From now on you'll room with her. She'll show you your duties." Neetha smiled and said hello. She wore a green tunic with a scarlet sash. She'd brought one along for Becky and laid it on the bed without a word. Stepping back she smiled again, a shy and friendly smile, then retired to the corridor while Becky washed and changed.

Walking out of that dingy room fresh and well dressed was the best moment she'd had in Longdreth so far. Neetha didn't say much but led her down flights of stairs through corridors with narrow slits in the wall, then out into sunlit halls where the windows were wide and open. By one of these they paused.

A fresh breeze blew in, bringing a taste of the sea and cries of distant gulls. The view was breathtaking. Many stories above the ground, they looked out toward the giant bridge crossing the river. From here Becky could see just how large the city was, spreading out to where the wall circled it on the south side of the river. Beyond that far line lay green fields, dykes, and roads. And beyond these, a blue fringe of forest. Below her huddled hundreds of houses built of stone and wood, reflecting in their design the standing stones precious to the Rock Movers. On many doorposts was carved the figure of a ram.

The streets teemed with hundreds of people, animals, and carts. Pavilions and awnings of bright cloth flowered in narrow alleys. Where main streets crossed, bazaars bloomed, spilling over with fruit, vegetables, pots, skins, sheep, goats, bolts of cloth, and the hundred-and-one other things people buy and sell. From where she stood, the noise of the crowds sounded like the murmur of an ocean, broken now and then by the singsong cry of a vendor or bray of a donkey. Near the river rose an open theater with seats for thousands. On a high platform in the middle of it sat a statue.

"What's that?" she asked, pointing. Neetha's eyes fell and the corners of her mouth turned down.

"That is Phogros," she answered. At that very moment the sun passed under a cloud and they heard a far-off shriek. Above the bridge, two clumsy birds beat at each other, fighting over one of the black knobs Becky had noticed before. Neetha shuddered and turned away.

· *Longdreth* ·

During the next few days Becky learned much about the city of the Rock Movers. Neetha was a better source of information than Brieda, as well as a better friend. Her shyness soon wore off. Desperate to learn where they had imprisoned Cavallos, and to figure out a way of escape, Becky questioned her about the centaur. Neetha knew little but said Targ was likely to keep Cavallos alive until a major feast day. That gave Becky a little hope.

The two worked together cleaning rooms and setting out the bedding. Laundresses carried it away in the morning and returned it fresh at night. At other times the two picked up a list from the palace kitchen and shopped for fruit, spices, and other delicacies. They were followed on these outings by an old and deaf palace guard, who pulled a little cart to carry their purchases.

One morning they left the kitchen by the back door

and passed through an alley. On one side frowned barred windows, low to the ground. "I think your friend may be in the dungeons there," Neetha whispered, glancing warily back at the guard. Becky stared at the grills, but could see nothing through them.

That day they threaded their way to the quays on the river where fresh fruit was sold. They shopped for strawberries, brought downriver by farmers, along with early raspberries and blackberries. Then they watched two jugglers and a tumbler, a dancing bear led by a man with one eye, and a group of traveling musicians, who played stringed instruments made from tortoise shells. The sweet aroma of fruit mingled with the smell of unwashed bodies and the ripe odors of animals. Now and then a skinny child gazed at their fruit with hungry eyes. Neetha always slipped him a piece if the guard wasn't looking.

As the singers finished, a high note sounded from a flute, and a man addressed the crowd in a strange tongue. Clothed entirely in red silk from his shoes to his turban, he stood in front of three small ships drawn up to the quay. The ships glistened with bronze and carved wood; their sails were candy striped in reds, blues, and yellows. The man pointed along the quay to baskets of oranges, lemons, limes, bananas, watermelons, honeydews, pomegranates, mangoes, and fruits Becky couldn't identify. Most of the crowd could not afford the prices, but watched the man in wonder. Neetha pushed forward to dicker, filling the cart with tropical delicacies. He stood over her, tall and swarthy, a tame monkey sitting on his shoulder eating an orange peel. The monkey wore a red turban like his master's and a little coat of green silk with gold buttons. His foot was attached to the man's wrist by a golden chain. From the bow of the first ship stared a large painted eye, entirely blue.

On the way back to the palace Becky asked where the ships were from. "Ack-Lonthea," Neetha replied. "It's a huge island to the west and many *hendar* south of here—in the Great Ocean. It is said that the Ack-Lontheans rule the world, that they have found the key to happiness."

"Why?" Becky asked, jumping over a gutter.

"They have ships that move even when there is no wind and chariots that move without horses. But mostly they have much gold and many precious stones with which they adorn their buildings. There winter never comes, and all spend their lives in music and dance. Even the slaves are more fortunate (it is said) than a free man here. But I think that is a lie. The Ack-Lontheans look down on all other peoples, and even Targ must listen to what they say.

"It is from them we Rock Movers learned how to move rocks, keep track of the days, and build many things. It is said that the Ack-Lontheans have so much wealth they give feasts lasting for weeks. At those feasts they try to outdo one another in giving things away. And, if one outgives the other, sometimes the other is so proud he will take his own life rather than suffer the shame."

Becky said nothing, but thought about this the rest of the way back.

As they passed by the dungeon windows Becky thought she heard a muffled groan. She paused by an open door just beyond the gratings. The deaf guard had gone ahead into the kitchen. Neetha turned and was about to speak, but Becky put her finger to her lips and motioned her on. Then she leaned up against the wall, as if resting. The moans continued and she heard a door slam somewhere inside. A voice yawned and exclaimed, "By the toes of Phogros, I thought you'd never come, Britt!"

"Why?" a sullen voice replied, "guard duty too rough for you?"

"It's that sack of dog meat, the horse-monster. Had him on the rack again all day. Couldn't get a thing from him. Even tried hot coals. He passed out on us."

Black spots swam before Becky's eyes. She steadied herself with one hand.

"Torture's blasted hard work," the other agreed, "even when you enjoy it. No one gives us credit for that—least of all, Targ."

"Ha, Targ!" came the first voice. "That's because he wants to do it all himself. I've seen him skin a satyr alive with one hand while eating an orange with the other." The two chuckled.

"At the sacrifice to Phogros . . ." the voices faded as the guards moved away. Becky felt sick to her stomach. She ran to her room, resolving to trust Neetha or die.

"I'll help you," Neetha promised after Becky explained. Her dark eyes shone. "And maybe someone else will, too," she added mysteriously. Each day was agony as Becky waited for a chance to free her tortured friend. Talking with Neetha kept her hopes up. But it was hard, especially the day she passed through the marble entry hall when the gates were open. Sun lit up the bronze plaques. She saw they told the story of the bloody conquest and extermination of faun, satyr, and centaur. Sickened, she returned to her room.

About a week later she was wakened in the night by a hand on her shoulder. Moonlight shone on Neetha's face, one finger at her lips. She sat up and her friend motioned for her to get dressed. The two slipped into the corridor lit by ghostly blue light from the windows. They crept down halls, pausing at each crossway to listen for guards. Finally, in a roomier part of the palace they came to a door of beaten copper. Neetha knocked softly—three knocks, followed by two. The door opened halfway and they slipped in.

Becky found herself in an ornate room with purple hangings on every side. Drawn back, one revealed a bed built into the wall. Above the bed was the sign of the ram. Bronze candlesticks stood everywhere, but only two candles were burning. To her surprise, in their light she recognized the pale face and glossy curls of Rhadas the Magnificent. His expression was totally different from that in the throne room. His mouth was drawn up in a smile. His black eyes sparkled.

"I'm so glad you made it," he whispered to both,

squeezing their hands. "Uncle Targ is drunk from this evening's banquet and will sleep for hours. There's much I've been wanting to ask you." He looked eagerly at Becky. "But first, let me say Neetha has told me of your fears for Cavallos. They are fears I share, and upon my honor as a prince I will do everything in my power to spare him my uncle's cruelty." His face flushed dark in the candlelight.

"Will you?" she looked up, "will you, really?" and hugged Neetha with all her might.

"You have my word!" he said gently.

The Prince motioned toward three ivory chairs. He offered each of them a gold goblet full of hot drink. To her surprise Becky found its taste familiar.

"You have chocolate!" she exclaimed before she could catch herself.

"Have you tasted it before?" Rhadas asked, surprised. Neetha and he looked at her with great wonder. Neither, of course, knew her true origins. They thought she was from among the First Ones.

Then the Prince proceeded. "Ever since I was a little boy I have loved tales of centaurs and other half-humans. My Uncle Targ and his cronies often spoke of them with cruelty or contempt, but my nurse and an old guard used to tell me wonderful tales of the woodland folk—of animals that could fly with men on their backs in the Golden Years before the world was broken—"

A heavy knock fell on the door. The three stared at each other. Waving Becky and Neetha behind a curtain, Rhadas opened it a crack.

"I'm sorry, Milord"—Becky recognized the voice

of the guard who'd dragged her off—"but I saw a light under your door and wanted to check that you are all right."

"I am!" said the Prince in an irritated and sleepy tone. "I'm just reading late." They waited until the heavy footsteps faded. When they spoke again it was in whispers.

"Then one day," the Prince continued, "the soldiers brought in an agéd satyr. His face did not look at all beastly, as the artists make the half-human look, but wise and sad. I managed to speak with him in the dungeons before he died, and he told me the truth about half-humans, how they were in touch with a wisdom our people had lost. Even more important, he told me First Ones survived in hills to the far west.

"What he said rang true to what I'd always felt since hearing tales in the nursery. I remember one little book lettered on silk and bound with silver. This book contained pictures every color of the rainbow along with stories and poems about the half-humans. It told of a faun who fell in love with the moon and sat pining for her every night. Once he fell asleep and a lady-faun with glossy silver flanks stepped down from the moon and placed by his side a silver pipe made from moon-metal. When he woke, he tried playing it. All the love which had filled the faun to bursting, until he had nearly died from it, came forth in the most beautiful music ever made. The rest of the wood people grew silent and listened. Later they said moonlight passed through it like silver.

"Every night the moon rose the faun would play

his pipe, and music like liquid moonlight wove through the woods. The faun took to being less and less seen. As time passed, his pipe could be heard only faintly, playing in the depths of the forest. Finally the music ceased and was heard no more by the other creatures. The rumor went about that the fauness pitied the faun and took him with her to the moon where in fields of argent he plays every night as she listens. It is said that on nights of the full moon, if you are very quiet, you can still hear him."

The Prince told this story with such feeling that Becky and Neetha sat charmed. When he finished, there was a long silence. Then with an eager look he turned to Becky. "But I want to hear from *you*. That is why I've called you here. Tell me of your friends the centaurs and your kindred the First Ones."

Although Becky now trusted the Prince, she thought it wise not to tell him her true origins. She admitted only that she had left her own people to live with the centaurs. She described in detail life among the centaurs, the history of the world as she had learned it from them, and what they had told her about the First Ones.

"You mean the First Ones are not afraid to die?" the Prince asked, in great awe.

"No, the First Ones see death as the end of life, for which all life prepares one," she said. "They see it as a door to another life, where what they have learned in this one will be used."

"My Uncle Targ is so afraid to die that he kills

anyone he suspects is his enemy,'' Rhadas said, frowning at the floor. ''I am taught that a king must destroy all his enemies so he might be rich and powerful. As he is rich and powerful, so will the Rock Movers be. I am told that the Ack-Lontheans once taught such lore as you have, but now they scorn anyone who doesn't live for riches and pleasure.'' He looked at the floor and sighed. ''To me, in this palace, life seems heavy and tedious, with all the talk of things and money. And worse, I am taught that half-humans are sorcerers and devils and must be destroyed. This very year my uncle hopes to exterminate the centaurs—most fierce of the half-humans. For it is they, and only they, who defend the others and make Rock Movers afraid of the forest.''

Becky's heart sank as she learned that the centaurs' fears were only too true. The Prince saw this and changed the subject. He spoke of his childhood and his longing to meet the First Ones.

The candles shone feebly in pale light from a window. They had talked the night away. The Prince snuffed the flames and told the girls to return the next night. Meanwhile, he would plan an escape for Becky and Cavallos. The two hurried through empty corridors in the growing light, much too excited to feel tired.

That night there was planned a special banquet for the Ack-Lonthean ambassador. Targ fell into temper for fear the menu would not please his guest and flogged the Master of Revels and three cooks when a dessert they proposed didn't please him. At the last minute, Becky and Neetha found themselves hurrying down to the quays to look for honeydew melons and four or five baskets of strawberries.

They found the Ack-Lonthean fruit vendor and his monkey in the same spot. He was talking with an even more impressive-looking foreigner in a gold shirt and pink turban fastened by a diamond. His face shone dark and handsome, and he wore a crisp black beard filled with rings. A jewelled sword flashed at his side. As the girls pressed forward to buy melons, his eyes widened. He laughed and said something in a foreign tongue, slapping the vendor on the back. Then he spoke to him in a low tone, glancing frequently at the girls, before turning and striding off. Becky felt uneasy.

As they looked over the melons, the vendor wheedled, "The Ambassador thinks you are very pretty girls. Such pretty girls should eat melons, no?" He rubbed his hands and smiled widely. The monkey imitated his master, rubbing its little hands and chattering. So, Becky thought, that was the Ack-Lonthean ambassador!

They had little time to enjoy the compliment, however, for they had to help the guard push the heavy cart uphill to the palace. Only the larger streets were paved, and often the cart bogged down in mud. They arrived back at their room sweaty and smudged.

Brieda was waiting for them, looking sourer than usual. "Targ says you both are to bathe and dress for the banquet tonight. He's sent along some dress clothes, though I don't know why he'd waste silk on wenches like you!" she grumbled. "Mind, don't spot them, or he'll feed you to the ravens." She smiled a ghastly smile and thrust into their hands a pile of sweet-smelling, shiny material.

The bathtub was a sunken marble pool. Two servants poured hot water and crystals into it, scenting the whole room. It was a better experience than the cold shower they usually took. Bubbles rising to the chin felt heavenly. Soaps carved like exotic birds, each with a different fragrance, perched in silver dishes on the edge.

Afterward, Becky slipped into a pair of blue silk trousers and a white silk tunic embroidered with flowers and birds. A pink sash and dark blue slippers completed her outfit. Then a tall, huffy servant with silver fingernails wove bluebells in her hair. The pleasure of all this was shadowed by her worry that they not miss the meeting with the Prince.

A green-robed retainer led them into the throne room. The throne had been replaced by a buffet, gorgeous with foods. A rich scent blew from the fountain, perfuming the whole room. Small mechanical birds, activated by water, trilled and chirped among the real ones, which sang lustily to outdo them. In the room's center low tables waited, with a large silk cushion for each diner.

As they walked in the door, a retainer struck a gong and announced the Ladies Neetha and Becky. Targ barely nodded, but the Ambassador, on his right, greeted them with a fascinated smile. The rest of the company, lords and ladies of Longdreth, shone in dazzling silks of every hue, ornamented with rams and ewes, trees and birds, fruits and flowers.

Becky had never had such a feast in her life. Targ clapped his hands and three dancers appeared, flinging rose petals and scented water over the guests. Then retainers, all in green, brought everyone a sweet bubbly drink made of chocolate and cream, but not at all filling. This was followed by fruits and vegetables done up in the shapes of peacocks and served with cheese and hot breads.

Between each course waiters stooped before the diners with scented water and hot towels. Next came the soup, a golden broth she couldn't name, but very savory. The soup was followed by lobster and three kinds of fish served in dishes resembling the Ack-Lonthean ships. Everyone applauded and smiled at the Ambassador. After these came every meat dish imaginable, including a boar roasted whole with an orange in his mouth and dressed like a clown. (Becky thought he resembled Targ.) After this more salad arrived, and next, the sweetest pineapples imaginable. Then cheese with fruits. Then a ten-tiered chocolate cake designed like the palace. Again, everyone oohed and aahed. Finally, a bitter drink similar to coffee and trays of sweets. When they were done Becky groaned. She'd eaten too much and wondered if she'd ever stand up again.

Targ clapped his hands a second time. Servants came in, removed the tables, and replaced them with trays filled with wine and nuts. Then singers and dancers, a magician, and a group of tumblers performed.

The vendor and his monkey appeared—all in blue. The monkey strummed a tiny mandolin and looked so sad everyone laughed and threw coins. The monkey bowed and scrambled around, putting them up in his cap. But first he bit each coin to see if it were counterfeit, causing further roars of merriment. After he withdrew, music stole softly from an alcove while the banqueters talked.

Throughout this entertainment the Ack-Lonthean ambassador spoke earnestly with Targ. Becky noticed this as she now and then stole a glance at Rhadas, sitting on his uncle's left. The Prince appeared dull and expressionless—an act, Becky knew now. It bothered her that the Ambassador often glanced at her and smiled. She grew very uneasy.

At last, Targ clapped his hands a third time and commanded in a loud voice: "Becky of the First Ones, present yourself before us!" She was shocked. Had he discovered her visit to the Prince? Would he sentence her to death? Her knees felt like jelly and she imagined a hundred awful things as she stood and walked stiffly toward the high table.

"Pay your reverence to His Eminence, Faloor, Ambassador of Ack-Lonthea to the Court of Rhadas the Magnificent!" Becky made the low bow she'd been taught her first day as servant. Faloor's eyes sparkled like the jewels on his fingers. His teeth were very white and he smiled broadly.

"Faloor has honored you and my house by requesting your hand in marriage for his son Yasuf, heir to all his lands in the far splendor of Ack-Lonthea." Becky's jaw dropped. She was sure she'd misunderstood. But Targ continued, "You and Yasuf will not be joined in matrimony for many years, not until your education is complete and Yasuf has come of age. Yet you will depart for Ack-Lonthea with Faloor tomorrow."

The whole speech, especially the last word—*tomorrow*—went through her like a knife. Her skin felt numb and her feet too heavy to move. Was she to be carried off to yet another distant place and leave Cavallos to be skinned alive? Her tongue was paralyzed.

The smiling Faloor came to her aid: "It's too much for you to hear all at once, my child. If I could delay a few days, I would, but we must leave at dawn. Meanwhile, let me assure you, you will be very happy in Ack-Lonthea. I will treat you as my own daughter." He smiled kindly.

Becky knew enough about the Rock Movers, and especially Targ, to realize no protest would help. As far as they were concerned, she had been done a great and enviable honor. To gain a few hours of freedom—for she knew Targ might lock her up otherwise—she forced a smile and said with lowered eyes, "My Lord Faloor does me too great an honor. My heart nearly faints within me, but I give you great thanks." She had heard enough of this sort of speech at court to be able to use it now, though she felt uncomfortable deceiving the Ambassador.

Targ regarded her coolly for a moment, then smiled a fat and greedy smile. "Return to your quarters and pack. You will leave the palace in the morning with the Lord Faloor."

"Can you believe it?" Neetha asked, as the girls ran back to their rooms. "No doubt Faloor paid a fortune for you." Her eyes were wide with excitement.

"Oh, Neetha, of course I can't believe it! It means I've got to rescue Cavallos somehow and escape tonight. Will you help me?" Neetha's face fell and she looked away for a moment.

Then she said slowly, "We'll go to the Prince as soon as we can. He'll know what to do." She said no more as they pretended to pack Becky's few things for Ack-Lonthea. Becky guessed what was on her mind. To Neetha, it must seem as if she was throwing away the chance of a lifetime—to live like a princess in a fabulously rich country. After all, it was the stuff fairy tales were made of, and Neetha no doubt grieved as if she herself had been stopped from going. Yet, to her credit, she said nothing more about it.

The River Daughters

The banquet seemed to go on forever. It was one in the morning before the palace quieted down enough for the girls to creep to the Prince's chamber. Fortunately, the night was overcast and the halls dark. They found Rhadas very anxious, pacing up and down.

"There's no time to lose," he said urgently, as they slipped in the door. His face was pale. "I've learned Targ plans to kill Cavallos tomorrow night, at the Feast of First Harvest. I have a plan. Listen carefully."

He had duplicate keys to the dungeons, made after his friend the satyr's execution two years before. Tonight, after his uncle's announcement, he'd ordered wine sent to the dungeon guards—first excusing himself to his room for sleeping powders to put in it. These, he said, would cast them into a deep sleep for hours. Still, they could be wakened and Becky had to be careful. The important thing was to make no noise opening the outer and inner doors.

Becky would go alone to release Cavallos. Meanwhile, he would give Neetha sleeping powders too, so it would look as if Becky had drugged her companion and not had her aid. He would see that nothing happened to Neetha during his uncle's tantrum, bound to follow the escape of a prize captive. Rhadas then described the best way to the dungeons and made her repeat the directions twice. Since the city gates were guarded, he urged that Cavallos and she escape by the river, swimming under the grating where the water passed through the wall. "That is by far the safest way," he stressed.

When all had been explained, he looked at her sadly: "I hope when I am king I may see you again. Perhaps our peoples can live at peace, and I can visit the centaurs and the First Ones. They have much to teach me." Neetha threw her arms around her and burst into tears.

Her eyes misting, Becky promised to ask they be allowed to visit—if she made it back to Silver Garth. But her heart was heavy with foreboding. She said she hoped Rhadas would be as good a king as he was a prince and undo the misery his uncle had caused and that Neetha would marry whomever she willed. All three hugged silently and Becky slipped into the dark corridor.

It was cold. She was glad she'd changed into her own jeans and shirt. She felt in her pocket for the keys and the small knife the Prince had given her. Every few yards she paused, listening for footsteps in the murky corridors. Occasionally snoring drifted from behind a door. At the first turn she froze. A dark figure loomed above her, holding a spear. A full minute passed before she realized it was a statue.

Once she nearly tripped over a body in front of a door. "That must be Targ's bedroom and his guard," she thought, shuddering as she tiptoed by the sleeping form. She had to turn seven times and go down five flights of stairs before reaching the level of the dungeons. Once there she carefully counted and recounted stairs and turns to be sure. At last, after an hour, she stood in front of a wooden door with an immense iron ring. Her heart in her mouth, she felt for the larger of the two keys.

Holding her breath, she inserted the key in the lock. Fortunately, it turned easily with a light clinking of tumblers. Then she tried the great iron ring. It moved with difficulty but finally gave. Inch by inch she opened the door, avoiding the squeak the Prince had warned her about.

The opening yawned dark and cavernous. Stale air greeted her nose. She could see nothing. Gingerly she edged forward. Her toe met something soft and she jumped back. She heard a grunt followed by a snore—it was a guard sleeping in the doorway. She nearly panicked as he rolled over and settled on his other side, his hand brushing her leg. Gradually her eyes made out his figure in the semi-darkness. At the bottom of the dim stairs a shadow wavered. Apparently there was some sort of light down there. She drew the door almost shut behind her and, still holding her breath, tiptoed over the sleeping form.

After twenty steps or so the stairs turned sharply to her left. There in a wall socket, burning low in the foul air, was a single torch. It threw a fitful light over a narrow corridor reaching into shadow, where someone snored loudly. Straw covered the floor. It stank. On her left stood many doors with tiny grates in them. Cavallos lay behind one of those, but which one?

She hurried to the first and, standing on tiptoe, looked in. All dark. "Cavallos?" she whispered. There was no answer. "Cavallos!" she risked again, this time louder. She heard a groan and someone stirring, then silence. She moved on to the next door. "Cavallos!" she said as loud as she dared. Nothing. She tried again—no response.

She was about to take the torch out of its bracket to help her look when she heard a weak but familiar voice: "Over here—the fourth one!"

Her heart nearly burst as she rushed to the fourth door, hand fumbling for the key. A click, and the door opened. Before her stood the vague figure of her friend.

He blinked in the dim light. Neither spoke. He looked paler than she remembered, and thinner too. His beard was matted and hair hung limp over his forehead. But his eyes flashed like dark coals.

"Becky!" he exclaimed, and pressed her to his broad chest.

"Are you all right?" she gasped, breathless in his hug.

"Yes," he said. "How did you . . . but we can talk later. Lead on!"

She warned him of the sleeping guard. They started quietly up the stairs, Becky in the lead. The flickering torch threw giant shadows on the wall as they climbed. It was a sight to trouble the dreams of anyone, and perhaps it troubled those of the guard, for he moaned twice and turned over as the hoofs of the centaur lifted one by one over his head.

After locking the dungeon door behind them, they crept ten paces left, where a small door led to the kitchen alley. Quietly Becky drew the bolt. Though overcast, the sky outdoors looked too bright after the dungeon murk. They hesitated a moment, then slipped into the street, shivering with the joy of their new freedom.

The alley led downhill. It was walled, with no windows except the black squares of the dungeon grates. Behind them it came to a dead end against the kitchen. No one from the palace could see them, except for the other prisoners, if they had climbed up to the grates, which was unlikely. The real danger was of someone's coming along the street, a good block away.

Softly, because the centaur's hoofs echoed, they moved toward the alley entrance step by step. Fifty feet from it Becky caught her breath. A light flickered against the far wall of the street facing the entrance. She heard footsteps coming. They must belong to the night watch! It was too late to move back to the shadow of the palace door. Their only chance was to hug the wall and hope no one looked. The footsteps rang louder. As they flattened against the wall, a torch bobbed around the corner and nearly into Becky's face.

"Becky!" a surprised voice exclaimed. "What are you doing here?" There in the torchlight, his huge face screwed up in a grin and his eyes laughing, stood Tull, carrying the staff of a night watchman.

Becky and Cavallos both put fingers to their lips. Tull's big face fell in a frown.

"Cavallos, you too? Why are you out in the middle of the night?"

"Listen, Tull!" Becky tugged at his sleeve, "Do you know they are going to kill Cavallos?"

The giant man looked confused, and his frown deepened to a scowl. "Kill Cavallos! Why?"

"Because Targ hates him and Targ is a murderer. I am helping Cavallos escape before Targ can do that. Will you help?"

Tull stood for a long moment in the bright torch. All too bright, Becky thought. It was lucky there were no windows.

Then his face cleared. A big smile spread across it. "Tull does not want Cavallos to die. That would make Becky sad. I will help. But you can't go out the gate—many guards." He held up all his fingers, shaking his head.

"We'll go by the river," Becky said.

"Can you swim?" Tull asked, surprised. Then his expression grew ridiculously crafty. Another time Becky might have been tempted to laugh. He put his finger to his mouth, narrowed his eyes, and glanced about. "Yes, the river will hide you. Good! But others will see Cavallos on the way to the river.'' He paused, straining to think. Suddenly he laughed out loud and clapped his hands. ''I will give him my cloak. He will then look like just a horse.''

Quickly they threw the cloak over Cavallos. The centaur bent over as far as possible, with his head wrapped. In the dark he looked indeed like a horse with a very long neck.

Becky thanked Tull and hugged him tight. The big man strode on, swinging his lantern and turning to wave every few steps. Only when he disappeared at the next corner did they dare step from the protection of the alley. As they moved down the street toward the river, they heard his big voice boom in the distance, ''Three o'clock and all's well!''

Down street after street they moved, seeing no one. Still, on both sides shuttered houses loomed up, unfriendly. Becky was soon soaked with cold sweat. As they drew close to the river a party of revellers tottered toward them. Becky and Cavallos drew back into the shadows, but fortunately the group turned into a house a half block from them.

They'd sighted the dull gleam of the river when a figure lurched from a doorway, slipped, and fell down under Cavallos. He looked up directly under the cloak and scrambled to his feet. ''Phogros! A centaur! What will it be next?'' they heard him mumble as he staggered up the street from side to side. In his haste he dropped an empty wineskin.

The quays were deserted. They descended stone stairs to the river's edge and followed a narrow path east, downstream. Here under the bank they were out of sight of the houses, and anyone on the river itself would hardly pause to question them. However, looming over them was the shadow of the great bridge. If anyone looked down from one of the houses on it, he could see them, but it was unlikely he would climb down to question a figure with a horse. Looking up, Becky saw a pair of black wings land on one of the knobs she'd noticed before. Cavallos followed her look upward.

"What are those knobs, and what is that bird doing there at night?" she asked.

Cavallos paused. "Those," he said in a hoarse whisper, "are the heads of Targ's enemies." As they passed under the shadow of the bridge they heard a harsh shriek from above.

The skin on Becky's neck crawled as they emerged on the other side. As long as they were in sight of the bridge, she felt the death-bird's eyes upon her. At last the river bent, and they were out of view. Before them loomed the lesser shadow of the city wall. This she knew was really the more dangerous obstacle because of the guards manning it. Their one hope was that all of them would be looking outward.

A dim, half-moon shape shone in the wall. It was the culvert through which the river flowed. Across it an iron portcullis showed its teeth little more than a foot above the water. Somehow they must swim or float under those iron spikes. But how could they, without alarming the guards?

Cavallos stopped and whispered, "See if you can

find a small boat hereabouts." She didn't see how a boat would help, but, leaving Cavallos in the shadow of the river bank, she crept ahead looking for one.

A pier ran out from the path. Two small boats bobbed at its end. One was tied so tight she couldn't undo it. The other's rope was knotted too, but smaller, and she cut it with the Prince's knife. Slowly she towed it back to the centaur, careful not to scrape it against the bank.

"We'll have to go back," he whispered, "out of sight of the bridge."

Once around the bend Cavallos lowered himself into the water up to his neck. He held the boat while Becky followed suit. It was cold and she wanted in the worst way to kick and splash but dared not. Quietly dog-paddling, she put one hand on the boat's edge, or gunwale. Quickly Cavallos explained his plan.

They kicked the boat out into midstream, hanging to its side. The sluggish current took it and carried them downstream toward the city wall. As best they could they kept their heads below the gunwale, out of view of the wall. When it passed under the culvert they swung the boat around so as to be out of view from the other side. The cold was almost unbearable, and waiting motionless in the slow current worst of all. She had to bite her tongue as the boat scraped the teeth of the iron grid and clunked against the stone wall.

"What was that?" said a sharp voice above them.

"What was *what*?" asked a sleepy voice.

They heard footsteps, and suddenly the water

flashed with light from a torch. They hugged the narrow shadow of the boat, now holding on by a rope that dangled over the side.

"Just a skiff loose from its moorings," the sleepy voice said.

"Shouldn't we retrieve it?" asked the sharp voice. Cavallos and Becky huddled closer.

"Nah," the sleepy voice growled. "Let the owner look for it in the morning! The bottom's rotten anyway. Look how it lists to one side."

The torch disappeared, but they drifted in the same position for five long minutes before daring to move. Then Becky felt a cold puff of air. Turning her head, she glimpsed four brilliant stars through a rift in the clouds. Without a word she and Cavallos started kicking downriver.

It was a mile or more till they were out of sight of the wall. The breeze freshened, smelling of the sea. As they rounded a bend, she looked up and saw the sky nearly half stars, large, liquid, and warm. Despite the cold, her heart stirred. The clouds moved on west and in a minute the waves' small teeth glittered under a yellow moon.

"Nearly at the full," Cavallos broke the silence. "It would have been this coming night," he added mysteriously.

"What would have?" she asked.

"My execution at the Moon of First Harvest," he smiled grimly. Again they were silent.

The boat rounded the bend and floated along beds

of tall reeds. Becky thought she heard the wind whistling among them. But it was more of a humming noise than a whistle. Then she made out the beginnings of a melody but couldn't be sure. Now and then the tops of the reeds quivered, followed by a gurgling and a high watery laugh. She looked at Cavallos.

"Shh," he said, his eyes bright. "It's the Daughters of the River Temenos—the naiads. They sing."

Soon Becky heard what she never heard before or again in that country—the song of the River Daughters. First it sounded like humming, but a hum made up of all the watery sounds of a river. Then she made out a pattern, a melody. It seemed to swell and lap with the current and the movement of the wind. It rose to a high pitch, telling the secrets of the river, of the clear fountain where it was born and the laughing tributary streams; then, in a lower voice, of still inlets where furry and shy creatures lived, of green tunnels blocking out the sky and shedding myriad leaves on it in the fall. Next a chorus of voices sang of huge rocks it threw itself over in roaring cascades and of broad fields it curved through under the moon; then a solo voice told of farmers' daughters who combed their hair by it, looking longingly at their reflections, and of farmers' sons who would lie daylong by it and dream. Finally, deep tones told of the great city which tried to control it between stone banks and of marshy plains where it spread out free again. But above this and through it all, ran one unmistakable note—the unutterable longing of the river for the sea.

Becky didn't know how long it lasted. But when the song stopped, she thought she could hear, far off, the rhythm of waves on sand. Only then did Cavallos turn into the reedy shore.

The Moon of First Harvest

They hid the boat well in the reeds and started off through swampy lowlands south of the river. To their left the sky shone pearly gray. The air felt colder than the water. Mud oozed above Becky's ankles and reeds lashed her face.

"Climb up on my back," Cavallos urged. The centaur's body, though wet, was warm and steaming in the early morning cold. Fortunately the colder air brought fog up from the marsh, and in a few minutes they were hidden from view. Without the fog, they would be visible for miles in that treeless landscape.

In half an hour they came to a wide track paved with bundles of reeds. Recalling their capture on a public way, they moved along it cautiously, stopping every few minutes to listen. In the growing light, Becky saw how much Cavallos had suffered. His back was crowded with pink scars where lash wounds had gone untreated. His skin was pale from the dungeon and his body thinner. She could count the ribs of his human chest and feel his horse ribs between her knees.

A shout drove them into the high reeds. As they peered between them, a group of five fishermen trudged out of the fog, laughing and joking. They carried heavy nets over their shoulders to cast all day where river and ocean mixed. In a few seconds the fog swallowed them again. Later when the shadowy outline of three huts rose up, Cavallos swerved into the reeds again, cutting a wide circle around the village. On its far side the track climbed, and they found themselves in a lane with high banks covered with blackberries and gorse.

There had been no chance to bring food along, so they breakfasted on ripe berries. With one hoof Cavallos dug up a yellowish root and scrubbed it with wet leaves. The inside was breadlike, almost sweet to the taste. The centaurs called it goatshorn. Cavallos carefully filled in the hole he'd dug.

As they continued uphill a bright spot appeared in the sky. The sun was trying to burn through. Cavallos broke into an easy gallop.

"We want to be among trees when the fog clears," he said, but at the top of the rise, they galloped right out of it. Cavallos stopped. To the east, the sky blushed pink, with here and there a ghost of fog dragging its feet over fields and strips of woodland. South, the fields faded to a blue haze, except for smoke from an occasional village or farm. To the west, pastures climbed the sides of low hills.

"We want to go south a long ways before heading

west," he explained, "to avoid passing close to the city." The lane soon joined a road, so they squeezed through a hedge, crossed a field, and put a second, zig-zagging hedge between them and it. They followed a course mostly south and a little west, keeping the hills on their right.

As the sun grew hotter and the dew dried off, gangs of laborers came out to cut the yellow wheat. Cavallos and Becky hid when necessary and picked their way along wooded strips. He had on Tull's cloak, but a strange horse moving through the fields would still be an object of curiosity to local farmers. After one close brush with a group of three women carrying sickles, they looked for a place to spend the day.

Where two hedgerows crossed, they came upon a large grove. They plunged into it, relieved. Most of the oaks were covered with ivy, but the ground underneath was unusually clear. Soon the trees opened to reveal the familiar standing stones of the Rock Movers. Seven of the stones stood in a circle, lintels across their tops. In the center lay another stone, on its side, stained with something dark. They heard flies buzz and smelled a sickening odor.

Cavallos' face tightened. "No, not here," he said and quickly left the clearing. The sun hid under a cloud and the ivy-hung trees passed dull and menacing. In the greenish gloom it seemed as if the stones were feeling out their presence among the leaves. They hurried south, out of the grove.

When he had slowed to a walk, Cavallos said, "That place is bad. The very trees have soaked up the evil done there." His face flushed. "Thus have Rock Movers darkened every place where the First Ones danced with the woodland creatures."

They crossed four or five more fields and came finally to a wide place in the hedge. There, hidden from prying eyes, they stretched out and immediately fell into an exhausted sleep. The sun climbed steadily overhead and bees buzzed loud in the red loosestrife. Later, as it coasted to the west, a party of returning harvesters sang, unaware that their song mingled with the dreams of a centaur asleep in the next hedge.

A few stars shone when Becky woke, her throat dry and cracked from thirst. Something moved a few feet from her. The wide liquid eyes and twitching nose of a rabbit regarded her, its ears forward, perplexed by these strange visitors. She spoke and it turned, but didn't run. Then Cavallos moved a leg and it fled in terror.

"We have slept ten hours," he said. "More than we could afford!" On the south side of the hedge, a little spring trickled into a ditch. They drank from it, then washed. In the ditch Cavallos found leaves of what smelled like mint. He gave some to Becky, who chewed them hungrily.

"The juice will take the edge off your hunger," he said.

In the thickening dusk they started across a newly reaped field, sharp with stubble. Two hedges further on, they counted smoke from five chimneys in a little hollow to their right.

Although it was risky, they decided to investigate,

to see if news of their escape had reached this far. A belt of trees provided cover within fifty yards of the first cottage. From the talk and laughter within, they guessed it was a tavern or public house. A horse and donkey munched from a trough outside. Light streamed from open shutters onto the road they had earlier avoided. In the fading light, Becky crept to the window. If seen, she'd no doubt be mistaken for one of the local children running here and there, playing games between supper and bedtime.

From the window she could see clearly into the cottage. An oil lamp above the fireplace lit a white-washed wall and a broad trestle table. Four or five red-faced men were gathered around a pale fellow with a beard, eagerly listening.

"—and the gatekeeper shouts, 'I don't give a fig for your money. Go right on through!' " the pale man said, leering. The others threw back their heads and guffawed; two beat the table with earthen tankards.

"Well, yer honor," one of them asked, blowing his nose and wiping it on his sleeve, "what else goes on in the big town these days?"

The stranger smiled and raised a tankard to his lips, swallowing a long draught. His Adam's apple bobbed at each swallow. "When I left yesterday," he said, "they were getting ready to flay and roast a centaur that tyrant Targ had captured."

"You mean sump'n what *looks* like a centaur!" a thin man said, with a snort. The others exclaimed and murmured.

The visitor, obviously enjoying the attention, belched and stared at him. "That's what *I* thought too. Targ is, after all, a liar. But I paid one *crokar* and saw the beast, plain enough, in the palace dungeons."

"Yah, and he could have your tongue cut out for calling him a liar," the thin man sneered. But the others nodded with excitement and drew close while the traveler described Cavallos' appearance, exaggerating his size by half and adding horns. A farmer refilled his tankard.

"The Moon of First Harvest's a good time for a flayin'," said a fat man with three chins, smacking his lips and blowing the foam off his beer. "Let's hope the weather holds." That brought more remarks on the weather, a warning from one that they oughtn't delay in getting out themselves, and general head-shaking over the price of firewood.

A dark man with black hair growing from his ears spat in the fireplace: "Some of these victims nowadays ain't worth the wood to burn 'em."

Becky crept back to Cavallos and told him all she'd heard. With a snicker she asked what had become of his horns. He laughed. "Well, at least news of our *escape* hasn't come this far. Still, people now know there's a centaur in Longdreth, and, if they see us, might put two and two together."

The moon had come up and her silver light winked through the leaves as they threaded their way south in the shadow of hedgerows. This night was colder than last, the stars above bright and hard edged. The hint of fall that often haunts early August was in the air. All the insects in the world woke and sang to the full moon as she climbed toward the zenith.

Hour after hour they walked in a dream, punctuated here and there by light from a distant cottage. When they must cross an open field, Cavallos galloped full speed. The moon travelled south with them, and it was hard to believe the noisy crowds of Longdreth and Targ's foul dungeons could exist in so quiet and beautiful a world.

Becky was nearly asleep when Cavallos stopped.

"What is it?" She sat up.

"Shhh," he said. They listened. Far ahead and very faint, she heard a long, heart-rending wail.

"There it is again!" Cavallos exclaimed. "It seems to come from the top of that hill." Becky shuddered. All evening they'd moved closer to the hills, and now the first of any size—still fairly low—lay across their path.

Without warning a light burst from its top. They saw a brief tongue of flame and a rush of sparks heavenward. The sparks were followed by a roar of many voices. The moon stood nearly overhead.

"They must be celebrating the Moon of First Harvest," Cavallos said softly.

"We can skirt the bottom of the hill," Becky suggested.

"Yes, we can. And yet—" he broke off.

"Yet what?" Becky shivered, afraid of his answer.

"Yet, if it hadn't been for you and Rhadas, *I* would have been the victim at such a ceremony. I feel we must try to save whoever or whatever made that scream.''

And so began a night Becky never forgot. Swiftly they crossed the field into the trees at the foot of the hill. Slowly, tree by tree, they climbed to the top. Here the underbrush had been cleared away, and when close enough, they saw red flames flickering between the trunks. Keeping to the shadows, they crept closer. Soon they heard a rhythmic chant, a low drone, and glimpsed grotesque shadows passing between them and the fire. They couldn't make out any words except the repeated name, ''Phogros.''

The last tree was still twenty yards from the fire. Leaving Cavallos, Becky crept behind it. On the far side of the fire stood a group of men, women, and children in ordinary dress, except for a mark on their foreheads and holly in their hair. They were staring at something with great interest.

Becky jumped when she saw what they were watching.

Naked, except for leaves about the hips, seven tall men danced around the fire. One side of their bodies glistened blood-red; the other, black. The black and red paint divided them from their toes to their scalps, and the whites of their eyes shone hideously. Their hair, red and black to the waist, whirled madly as they danced. Each clutched a stone knife and chanted, raising it whenever he muttered the name of Phogros.

After a while Becky noticed something else. Next to the fire, on a low stone, lay a small bundle, mostly rope. Horns stuck out of one end and little cloven hoofs out of the other. "A sheep," she thought. "They're sacrificing a sheep." Then the horns lifted and, as a log burst, she glimpsed a resigned and terribly sorrowful human face.

Stumbling back into the shadows, she gasped the news to Cavallos. "I was afraid of that," he said, his voice cool and even. "They've found a faun." Quickly he outlined a plan.

They moved quietly around the hilltop to a point directly opposite and about fifty yards below the top. On the way Becky took out her knife and tested its sharpness. From the new spot, they heard the frenzy increase. "There's no time to lose!" Cavallos whispered.

Putting his hands to his mouth, his chest expanding far beyond a man's, he called out in a deep and frightening voice, "I AM PHOGROS! I AM PHOGROS!"

The revel above came to a sudden halt. "I AM PHOGROS!" he repeated.

A high, almost feminine, voice shrieked, "Kill the blasphemer!" With a roar and a flicker of torches the crowd crashed down the slope toward them. Cavallos, Becky clinging to him, slipped quickly around the hill toward their original hiding place. The crowd, as he had gambled, hurried down the far side and spread out over the fields, looking for the "blasphemer."

From behind the tree, they saw that five priests had left with the crowd. Only two now stood above the victim, watching the moon and chanting under their breath. Cries of "There he is!" and "This way!" floated up from below, answered by others of, "I see him!" and "Over here!" Soon the crowd would return. They must act quickly.

The priests now stood silent over the stone, their eyes wide and unseeing, waiting for the precise second the moon would cross the zenith. From one's mouth a little foam trickled white in the moonlight. Slowly they raised their knives high over the victim.

"Now!" Cavallos said under his breath, and charged. "I AM PHOGROS!" he shouted, halfway across the clearing. Amazed, the priests turned to find a centaur bearing down on them. They staggered back as Cavallos reached down and snatched up the faun. As he whirled about, one shrieked and with both hands thrust a crooked knife at Becky. Cavallos' hind hoofs lashed out. *Thud,* one caught the priest in the middle and his knife flew into the fire. With a cry the other priest turned and ran. Cavallos let that one go and rushed headlong down the hill the way they'd come. At the bottom he raced across the field without pausing, the faun still in his arms.

"There they go—on a horse," a voice cried out. Becky saw the sparkle of a torch behind them to the right. Cavallos jumped the first hedge, turned a sharp left, and began a wild zigzagging detour around the hill, far ahead of their pursuers. Becky hung on for dear life. After three fields, the farm land gave out and they found themselves in a moonlit beech wood by a stream sparkling among boulders. Cavallos waded in and climbed upstream to avoid leaving a scent.

After a half-hour, they paused to listen. There was no sound of pursuit. Breathing hard, he put down the faun by a moonlit pool, and Becky dismounted to untie him.

"Bless you! Bless you!" was all the faun would reply to their questions as he rubbed his limbs, sore and stiff from the ropes. "Ah, that was a close one, that was!" He kept looking to every side, as if he couldn't believe they weren't surrounded by enemies.

For the fourth time, Cavallos repeated, "Who are you and how did they catch you?"

"I hope nivver to come that close again," the faun said, rubbing the hair on his flanks. He cocked his head and stared at them for a long while.

"You're deserving to hear it," he said at last, hanging his head, "though my good mother told me never to speak with the four-hoofed or two-footed kind." A tear glittered on his cheek. "Ah, if only I'd listened to my poor loving mother!" He wept uncontrollably for a few minutes. Cavallos put a hand on his shoulder.

The faun looked up through his tears and smiled. "Such a moon tonight!" he said. "Who would have thought I would perish on a night like this!" and sobbed again.

"But you haven't!" Becky exclaimed, exasperated. "At least not yet."

By dint of much patient questioning, Cavallos and Becky managed to calm the faun and to piece together his story. He'd been one of a nutting party that ventured out of the wild wood to collect the still unripe acorns favored by the fauns. They'd dared to search for them on the hill sacred to Phogros.

"I sneaked off from the party to have a bit of a snooze," the faun winked, "and went to sleep under an ash. When I woke, I was surrounded by the two-footed kind. They held hooked knives at my chin." The party of reapers had bound and imprisoned him. At the memory, he snuffled loudly.

"Do you know these hills then?" Cavallos asked, changing the subject.

"Aye, I was raised in them," the faun winked again and then, suddenly suspicious—"Why d'ye want to know?" Cavallos explained that their only chance was to hide deep in the hills before they were tracked to this spot.

"And if you don't wish to roast, we'd better hurry!" Cavallos added, not unkindly. At a whisk, the other was off.

Dorm (for that was his name) proved to be a reliable, if unusual, guide. He led them up the stream by leaping from rock to rock and then on a stony path that only his eye could follow. Last, he disappeared. When they'd nearly given up on him, he returned to lead them across the shoulder of a hill. Finally, squeezing between two rocks (at least Cavallos had to squeeze) the party entered a small dingle crowded with giant rowan and beech. The dingle had limestone sides. It was watchfully silent.

Dorm gave a low whistle. Suddenly the rocks were scrambling with fauns. They crowded around him, all speaking and laughing at once. A very fat female, with white hair on her head and haunches, shrieked and waddled over to him weeping. At that, all the fauns wept. Some threw dust in the air and stamped their feet, so mournfully glad were they that Dorm had returned. Only after this commotion had gone on for some time did they notice the centaur and human.

When Dorm had introduced his new friends and told of the rescue, the others cheered and formed a ring about them. They danced in a circle, moving feet and short tails so fast that Becky saw nothing but a moonlit flashing of hoofs. All was done to the skirl of pipes hidden in the rocks, sounding like the soul of a beech tree bleeding from a broken branch. The dance and music stopped. For a moment the trees sighed and rustled; Becky glimpsed a figure with pipes scurrying into a hole. The dingle was empty, except for themselves and Dorm.

"My people are very shy, and it *is* time to go on," he whispered. "Also, the trees tell us men follow." He led them out the other end of the dingle, down a ravine into a forest of solemn elms. The moon had set by the time they came to its far edge. To the south open fields grayed in the early light. They paused.

"Goodbye," Dorm sighed, and once again burst into tears. Becky tried to comfort him, but it was no use. She herself felt sad, though she'd known him only a few hours.

"Here," he said, handing her a small pipe of greenish wood. "Breathe on it lightly and it will play itself—especially in the moonlight." When she looked up again, he was gone. She and Cavallos stared after him wordlessly. A robin gave a sleepy cry, and they heard from far, resounding on a hollow log, the tattoo of little hoofs.

At last Cavallos turned away and said, "We must cross the field while we can."

That day, in a hollow overgrown with blackberry brambles, they slept even longer than the day before. At sunset they gathered berries, roots, and wild lettuce. These filled her stomach, but Becky still felt famished. The night was overcast, so they moved openly across fields, continuing south and a little west. Woods were more frequent now and farms smaller and wilder.

At dawn they came out of a wood. Before them, as far as eye could see, rolled the treeless downs. A south wind blew full in their faces the smell of the sea. Everywhere the heather glowed purple. They found a tall patch to stretch themselves out in and fell asleep, cushioned on the fragrant flower.

That night, under a waning moon, Cavallos galloped to the top of the downs. There Becky saw a sight that still haunted her dreams years later. They stood on top of enormously high cliffs, unearthly white in the moon. Waves below them moved toward the shore like glittering harpstrings. A long white line of surf made a soft, distant music. From where they stood at the edge, she followed the line of cliffs west and south. They bent out to sea and rapidly sank toward the water. From that point, a low neck of land stretched beyond sight.

"There is the neck of land our people crossed long ago," Cavallos said. "The sea swallows more and more of it as the ages pass. In many places now, the high waves drive across it."

"It's almost too beautiful—" Becky murmured, "I wish Lala could see it too." Cavallos smiled.

He turned and broke into a gallop along the high and scented downs. The seabirds shrieked above them as the salt smell mingled with the heather. The shadow of horse and rider raced before them on springy ground. They seemed to go on forever, the world rolling under hoofs suspended between moon and sea. At long last they stopped.

Below them a line of standing stones marked a road white as a ribbon. Every hundred yards the ribbon was cut by the dark shadow of a stone. Like sinister sentries, the line stretched as far as she could see.

They crossed at a walk, feeling terribly exposed and whispering, though there was no need. "This road runs straight from the neck of land to Longdreth and is patrolled," Cavallos said. Once across he leaped forward and galloped west until the stones were tiny dots on the horizon. The night continued beautiful as a dream, and several times Becky caught herself nearly falling asleep.

In the morning they made their way down to the beach. The cliffs stood lower now. The one fishing village they'd skirted was a good ways behind and this cove hidden from view by cliffs. Here they swam as the sun rose. The surf woke Becky up, flashing green, blue, and pink in the rising sun. Later she had a drink from a spring that fell down the rocks to a fringe of nodding green weeds.

Becky looked up to see Cavallos stooped over a tidal pool. With a cry of delight he straightened up, holding something yellow, round, and wriggling in each hand. Using a piece of flint and Becky's knife, he made a fire of driftwood and cooked the crabs. Her appetite further sharpened by sea air, Becky stuffed herself with sweet, juicy meat. Nothing had ever tasted better, not even Targ's delicacies. Afterwards they retreated between two boulders at the base of the cliff.

In midafternoon cries woke them. Looking out from the rocks they saw four boys swimming in the surf. Fortunately none came near their hiding place, though neither slept the rest of the day. After the intruders left, they warily climbed the cliffs. As they started along the top, they thought they heard a shout behind them, but could see no one.

They moved inland again. The woods were now tall forest and difficult to move through. They easily avoided the few farms and risked traveling by day. The oaks were gigantic and robed in ivy. Beech trees shot up like pillars of a giant temple. And hills, young, rocky, and jagged, towered to the clouds.

Once, as they were crossing a wide, treeless plain, they spied dark figures in the distance. As they drew closer, these turned out to be another ring of stones—

larger than any they'd seen outside of Longdreth—standing alone in the middle of a silent waste. The sun was setting behind them and the sky flushed, as if with blood. The closer they drew the more they felt an oppressive dread. They skirted the stones far to the right, but as they passed, something within them wanted to turn toward the ring. It was as if the stones whispered and beckoned to them. Walking itself became difficult. Becky closed her eyes and Cavallos gritted his teeth. They heard a low mournful sound as the stones sang to them of their great weariness, of how they wanted to lie down and give up, of how all things ended in blood and darkness.

Cavallos cried out and forced himself to a trot. At last the ring dwindled behind, and they approached a shallow river lined with willows. It was then they heard a shout to the rear. Looking back, they saw tiny figures on horseback racing toward them from the stones, shields flashing in the sun, arms and legs black and blood-red. Cavallos leaped toward the willows and plunged through them into the river, running far south in the shallows before climbing the opposite bank.

On the far side they lost any pursuers among the high jumbled rocks and hidden glens of a new range of hills. Sweating and breathless, Cavallos paused at last by a green pool under a waterfall.

They slept in a pine grove through which the wind sang all night a low, comforting tune, and Cavallos felt they could chance another fire. He made a paste from pine cones and baked flatbread on a rock, the first bread they'd had for four days. Tomorrow, he promised, they would reach Silver Garth. Becky lay awake worrying about Neetha, wondering what had happened to her and Rhadas after their escape. At last the song of the pines lulled her to sleep.

In the morning they came down into the land of rolling meadows and wild hedgerows she recognized as centaur country. Cavallos threw caution to the winds and raced homeward as fast as possible, pausing only to pick his way through woods and across narrow streams. Some of these last he jumped—with Becky's permission—as she clung tightly to his shoulders. All morning he galloped openly, and only after lunch did he look for one of the secret paths that wound to Silver Garth.

While the westering sun shot its last gold lance through the trees, they came upon two centaurs binding sheaves on the back of a third. "Cavallos! Becky!" the two cried out, and the sheaves tumbled to the ground.

"All in good time. All in good time," Cavallos said, laughing since they asked questions all at once. Leaving the grain, the four galloped toward the village. Cratos, a dappled gray, raced on ahead.

As they cantered down the familiar path, Becky spotted cooking fires through the beech trees and heard excited voices. A crowd had gathered at the edge of the village. As they came in sight, one pulled away from the rest and flung herself toward Becky. It was Lala.

Canthorn and Green Flute

For minutes they stood there speechless, hugging each other. Then something large and white and warm pushed between them. It was the soft nose of a horse.

"Rebecca!" she cried out in a broken voice and wrapped her arms around the mare's quivering neck. Rebecca nipped her shoulder gently and nickered over and over, as if trying to tell her something.

When all were through hugging and calm enough to talk, Senecos took Cavallos' arm, his old eyes shining. "Tonight we will have a feast to celebrate your return, and then we shall hear your story."

There was a roar of delight and centaurs began running in every direction. Some pulled in logs to the fire. Flames sprang up and reflected warmly off the woven roof. The scent of pine mingled with savory smells of meat. Others drew jugs of leaflight from barrels in the storehouses. Greenleaf tuned his harp and still others brought out musical instruments. The light, warmth, food, and friendship were too much after the lonely and half-starved trek of the past few days. Becky could hardly believe it; she felt she'd truly come home.

"Come to eat!" a deep voice called out from the end of the longhouse. On the table waited round loafs, herb soup, venison stew, and pitchers of leaflight and leafblood. Food had never tasted better. She reflected how welcome this simple food was, compared to the over-rich fare of Targ's table. Rebecca munched contentedly at her side. Lala, on her other, was too excited to eat and spilled over with talk.

"We thought you'd disappeared into thin air," she said. "I was furious you'd left me behind until we found out what really happened. Biana was terribly upset—which reminds me, you should see Rhuana's foal now!"

When they finished eating, Cavallos told the story of the kidnapping. Senecos and Scopas stood next to him, a grave look on the seer's face. Next, Becky told of Longdreth, the palace, and their escape. There was much interest in the ways of the city and the Ack-Lontheans, and cries of dismay at the cruelty and waste of Targ's court.

Scopas shook his head. "How far men are bent from their true nature!"

The story of Dorm evoked outrage (and not a little laughter at his humorous ways). With a long face, Flimnos came forward to tell how the troop of centaurs had run right past the crucial turn-off in the trail. When they didn't catch up with Cavallos and Becky, they stopped to wait for them to come back. After several hours, they suspected foul play and spent two anxious days searching for clues. At last they'd come across signs of the Rock Movers' horses, but the trail was cold, so they had returned gloomily to Silver Garth with the news.

Finally, Senecos spoke. The kidnapping had put an end to the hunting season. All the hunters had been called in to prepare to move. The tribe was in some confusion, because none knew what the First Ones had intended to tell them through Becky. Yet Scopas said they must prepare to move anyway. They must gather the harvest and be ready to flee at a moment's notice if the Rock Movers returned.

A week or so after the kidnapping, Rebecca had galloped into the village, covered with scratches and burrs, but none the worse for that. By retracing her trail part way, they confirmed what they already suspected: that Cavallos and Becky had been taken to Longdreth. The next day, a small party set out for the Rock Mover capital. They had watched the walls and gates of Longdreth day and night from the marshes and saw there was no chance for one centaur—let alone four—to enter the city. Their mission a failure, they were forced to return to Silver Garth. They had been gone two weeks.

Following these speeches, the harpist struck a loud chord amid the tootings, hootings, and groanings of wooden pipes. The centaurs' pipes were larger than those of other woodland peoples. Most were several feet long and curved according to the grain of the wood. Some forked in the middle and others boasted mechanical stops. Still others attached to skin bags pressed under the arm and gave out a wild, piercing noise.

The hair on Becky's neck rose up. The walls shook and the ground trembled beneath her. A low vibration climbed within range of hearing. In a few moments her head was filled to bursting with it. It brought tears to her eyes and flooded her with a mellow golden light such as she'd seen on a winter's afternoon. It breathed through her like spring air heavy with lilac, and reminded her of things old, far away, and sad. And then of things tremendously glad as she imagined infinite numbers of stars and planets reeling in a brilliant dance.

The sound came from outside the longhouse, from the village center. As she stood transfixed, the others, tears of laughter on their faces, moved out of the house toward a bonfire lighting up the sky. His profile black against it, a centaur blew on a horn at least fifteen feet long and suspended from two tree limbs. He paused.

"The canthorn," Lala explained. "It is blown only twice a year." When the centaurs had formed a circle about the fire, the long, low yearning sound began again. Becky never could describe all the registers of this unique instrument or all the feelings it stirred. Some were new to her; others went so far back into childhood she'd forgotten them. It seemed as if in this horn the trees themselves had found a voice and were singing of the long years of the earth, its blighting and its healing.

It started in again. Slowly, one foot after another, the centaurs began to dance. While she watched, Becky understood why painters and sculptors have always been enthralled by horses in motion. She had seen colts frisk on a fine spring day and horses rise up on their hind legs. And she had seen the colossal dance of trained elephants in the circus. But a sight at once so solemn and momentous, so fierce and rollicking, as centaurs dancing, was beyond her experience. Further, she understood now those few pictures of centaurs in battle she'd seen on old vases and canvases.

The ground shook from the pounding of hoofs. Hair and manes streamed wildly, eyes gleamed in the fire, and sweat glistened. There were grave moments when, arms folded and eyes fixed on other eyes, the human half of the centaurs seemed to stand still, while the horse half did a slow, complicated shuffle. There were glad moments running over with merriment and horseplay.

One red-haired centaur, called Danos, with freckles on his face, arms, and shoulders, stood up on hind hoofs and did a wonderful dance, romping for at least three minutes. The combination of mischief and fierce animal glee on his face grew so strong that Becky could hardly bear to look upon him. No wonder the Rock Movers feared meeting centaurs in open battle!

Faster and higher came the notes from the canthorn. Faster and higher leaped the centaurs, until, just as Becky thought they must drop, they gave a tremendous shout and abruptly stood still. There was laughing, backslapping, hugging, and cooling off with more leaflight. The tribe was exhausted. In a half hour all but the watch had gone to bed, and Becky fell into a dreamless sleep.

The next day dawned warm and glorious. For a while, Becky lay on her pine-bough bed, listening to the familiar noises of centaurs breakfasting, centaurs drawing water, and centaurs pulling hay wagons out to the fields. After a leisurely meal, she and Lala went to the river to wash her clothes, bathe, and sun themselves. They had much catching up to do, and Becky talked long of the city and the lives of Neetha and Rhadas.

"They seem like prisoners," Lala said, "surrounded by all those fine things and kept from the water and trees." Becky acknowledged this was true and shared her hope her friends would visit Silver Garth in better times. In the afternoon she put on dry clothes and they joined the reapers in the fields.

Singing as they scythed, four centaurs moved across one field, keeping perfect step with each other. Others gathered the wheat into sheaves and piled it high on the wagons. Still others pulled it into the village to be threshed and stored. This work was joyful for the centaurs—its slow steady rhythm in the hot sun interrupted for talk, horseplay, or a cool drink of water in the shade. They ate their lunch in the fields and left off long before the sun dropped behind the trees.

Back in the village, Senecos came up to her, smiling gravely: "Scopas the Seer has been gone all this day. I was worried and sought him in the High Place. There he is, stretched out, deep in Seeing. He said it is his last Seeing and that tomorrow, at dawn, you must go to him. It concerns you, the First Ones, and the fate of our people."

Becky sighed. This one day of freedom from care

had put Rock Movers and First Ones far from her thoughts. And now they were back again. Lala seemed to understand, for she smiled and said, "Come. Let's swim once more and eat. We have a whole evening ahead of us."

Though there was no canthorn or dancing that night, the feasting was, if anything, merrier. The rumor of Scopas' approaching death had spread among them, along with his desire to speak with Becky. When a seer died, his last Seeing often contained instructions for the tribe. After weeks of worry and indecision, such a prospect lightened their hearts. Also, the death of a seer was an occasion for great celebration and awe.

"It lifts the heart to heaven," Lala said that night to Becky. "He goes to smooth the way for all." In the laughter and talk, the singing and high poetry, Becky again forgot herself—along with yesterday and tomorrow.

The stars were still visible when Senecos wakened her. Putting a finger to his lips, he led her out of the house between the sleeping centaurs. They walked in silence up the grassy path to the High Place. The dew was cold and soaked Becky's feet to the ankles. They climbed to the glen where the centaurs gathered in wordless song, then up stairs in the cliff. On top, on plain turf from which the land fell on all sides, the aged form of Scopas lay. His beard sparkled where the edge of the rising sun caught the dew on it. His face was pale, his mouth open, and his eyes unseeing.

"Scopas!" Senecos exclaimed, rushing to feel his pulse. Slowly the jaws moved.

"Do not fear, Senecos, I am still alive. I have been drenched with Seeings. Leave the girl here. You have done what I asked." His mouth closed again.

"Remain with him!" Senecos whispered to Becky before turning down the steep steps.

For a while Becky sat in the sun and warmed herself, watching the still face. Peace, a deep content, fell on her with the sun's rays. Several hours passed, but they seemed very short while she gazed on the dew-laden grass.

Finally Scopas moved his eyes and lifted his head. "The Seeing is now complete," he said, with a faint smile, "and soon I can cross to be with my fathers." He motioned to her to draw closer.

"In my Seeing I was in a place where flowers never fade and leaves hang like green jewels. A great Light came over me and I could not look up. Soon, the Light said, I would be with my fathers, but first I must speak to my tribe.

"The Light said many things, but chiefly that you are to go at once to seek Menos of the First Ones—and the Singing Stone. You will know Menos by the expression on his face. You must leave tomorrow, for the time is short. Already the disobedience of others has delayed your mission more than a month. My heart misgives me you may not return in time with the message from the First Ones." His eyes darkened and mouth twisted to one side. "I saw fire and smoke and heard the wailing of children."

"But how will I find Menos and this Singing Stone?" she asked.

"Go west, as you did before. Only this time you must go alone, with your horse. Make your way through the cloven valley to the high cliffs by the sea. The First Ones expect you and will guide you, once you are in the hills. Do not hold back for anything." He paused for breath. "You will meet trials on the way. The path holds more dangers now, and you must face them by yourself." He stared right at her. "But I believe a strong heart will carry you through."

He paused again. "Then my Seeing changed. I saw a planet of the star called Alpha Centauri. There is much I do not know how to describe: blue trees that soar like cliffs in which hang houses with floors of grass and walls of flowers; water that falls for hundreds of miles; an ocean that sings and on whose floor dance sea girls in ever-changing colors . . .

"There, the First Ones never yearned for the Thing That Is Not. There none fell beside himself, to hate and fear himself and all other living things. There birds with human faces fly about the woods, and there live many other peoples we have never seen. A forest grows there with trees thick as twenty of ours. It awaits our coming.

"I saw other things—" his voice grew weak—"all the times we have lived in on this Earth and many things I am forbidden to tell. More I cannot say," his voice faded.

The talk had drained him. "Tell Senecos to return," he whispered with effort. "I have a word for him. As for you, Becky, spend this day and night alone in the forest, away from the village, and think about what I have said. Tomorrow, ride as fast as possible to the western hills. Alone!''

He raised one hand and placed it on her head. She felt a strange warmth pass through her. She looked shyly at his eyes, burning brightly. "Go now. I rest," he said, and shut them.

Becky returned to the village. Senecos had packed her things in a knapsack. She gave him Scopas' message, then went to Lala, who followed her into the woods. There the two talked for an hour and, for the second time, parted.

"How I envy you!" Lala said, with a toss of her shining hair. Her eyes glistened and she smiled. "To see Menos and the Cave of Many Colors and to hear secrets only the Wise Ones know!" But all Becky felt was a cold lump in her stomach.

Throughout the afternoon she sat under a rowan tree, mulling over the words of the seer. Bees buzzed sleepily. The rowanberries were ripening. Most often, she just sat and looked at the leaves or at the gleaming orange berries—as the centaurs had taught her to look: deeply, forgetting all time.

The sun set and a shrinking moon crept up to watch her. She opened her pack and reached in for the green flute—ivory in the moonlight—and put it to her lips. One note came out. She moved a finger: another followed. She made up a melody as she went along. It seemed to suit the night and the moon and to wind itself into the secret places of her heart. At last she stopped and listened. From all things a melody returned which cannot be heard by ear. She sat still and listened to it through the passing velvet hours of the night.

The Journey

She woke when the first sunbeam pried between the leaves. Her first thought was that she was back in Silver Garth and had the whole day to spend with Lala. With sinking heart, she recalled her mission. To avoid thinking about it, she got up at once, hurried to a spring and threw water on her face. After a cold breakfast, she put on her knapsack and stepped out of the wood, a little beyond the village. She heard a friendly nicker and the thud of hoofs.

"Well, you're up early!" She gave Rebecca an apple from her pack, munching another herself. She was glad she didn't have to go into the village to fetch the horse. Mounting, she looked back. The sun glittered from a thousand golden points on the dewy thatch.

"Goodbye," she whispered, and wrenching her head to the west, pushed her knees into Rebecca's ribs. How different this departure was from the first! The sun shining off wet fields reminded her of the happy days with Cavallos, Lala, and the rest. As she passed tree and field, those earlier mornings, so full of high spirits and good fun, flashed before her, more real than they seemed at the time. Sadly, she recalled how soon the company had been sundered. The thought made her shiver. The surrounding fields were silent, expectant, as if waiting for her. And what else might be waiting? Rock Movers? Or worse! She shook her head free of these fears and recalled Scopas' words. Surely the old seer would not have sent her alone if the danger was too great. But he had mentioned trials . . .

The sun overhead, she stopped by a river where they'd lunched before. But this time she didn't swim. She had a bit of the centaur bread, some cold meat, and a few mint leaves that grew along the bank. She showed the mint to Rebecca.

"Not bad, eh, Rebecca?" she asked as the mare plunged her head down for more. To keep alert in the drowsy afternoon she urged her on at a trot.

As shadows grew long, they found a snug place in a hedge between two wild hawthorns. From there she could look out without being seen. Tethering Rebecca, she gathered sticks and risked a small fire. (She'd become very good with flint and steel.) With supper she drank a small flask of leaflight Lala had sent along. The drink seemed to fill her with the sound of whispering hawthorn leaves, and soon she was asleep.

When she woke, the sun was already hot. That day she entered the rolling and deserted lands of the First Ones, patterned with hedges and groves. She came to the long alley of trees, the crossways, and the buried stone. The stone brought to mind the clod of dirt and the following day's capture. She felt the ancient trees watch her as she passed it by. Nothing was amiss this time, though the hand seemed to point west for her alone. That night she bedded down in the grove where she had seen the faun. Yet this time all was different.

She fell asleep fast enough. Whether through some magic in that grove or not, her sleep was troubled by dreams. She dreamt the trees swayed violently as the wind chanted through them—*Alone! Alone! Alone!* She half-woke to find a breeze had sprung up, turned over and went back to dreaming:

Trees scowled and moved slowly about her, roots thrashing, to reveal one of the Rock Movers' standing stones. As she looked at it, the stone turned into a frightening, pale old man, whose mouth moaned in the shape of an O. The earth parted under him, and she saw a black cave. She watched roots writhe within and smelled an odor of decay. Last, she was drawn into the cave, which closed over her head with a crash. She screamed and woke up.

All about her it was still. She forced herself to close her eyes, and the dream trees loomed again, this time painted bright colors and holding knives while they chanted. When she woke a second time, the sky was graying.

She got up but couldn't shake the mood of her nightmare. The trees looked unfriendly in the gray light of dawn. Munching bread from her sack she thought of the old man in her dream and then of the Cave of the First Ones. What if the First Ones had duped the centaurs all these years? What if they were really the crazed old men the Rock Movers said they were? Maybe they wanted her alone in order to sacrifice her as the priests tried to sacrifice Dorm.

At this thought the dry bread stuck in her throat. She shivered uncontrollably and looked out of the grove. Sunlight shone on the hills to the west—so much closer now. They looked like huge and jagged teeth. The sparse land leading to them offered little cover. She couldn't go on. She'd go back to the centaurs and plead to return to her own time through the Eye of the Fog. She was too young for this sort of thing. They'd understand. Lala would help her escape. A breeze sprung up and all the trees nodded their branches, *Yess, Yess!*

She put on her pack and ran east, out of the grove. When she stepped into the sun, she felt its warmth on her legs. She lifted her face. The sun cleared her head of the fears of the grove. Her mood shrank to a small, brown blot and fled back under the trees.

Why of course, she realized, the First Ones were good because the centaurs knew them—and the centaurs were good! Even legends among the Rock Movers told her that, especially the ones she'd heard from Rhadas. Then she thought of Targ and how wicked he was and shuddered. But she'd never been afraid of him the way she was afraid in that grove. Why?

She looked back at its shadows, now dissolving in the rising sun. Could this be one of the trials Scopas had warned her about? Was it a test of some sort? Were there things even in nature that didn't want her to finish her mission? She recalled the black stag with red eyes. What was it that men feared so much they turned to bloody idols like Phogros? The thought was too big to follow just now. She shook her head and turned west.

The hilltops now looked as inviting as pink clouds on a summer morning. All she had to do was go there. There was journey's end. Thumbs under her knapsack straps, she strode to where Rebecca calmly cropped the long sweet grass.

That afternoon she entered the hills and bathed in a cold stream with buttercups on its bank. Rebecca cooled her legs in it. Refreshed, they climbed a low hill and spent the night between stone slabs leaning together like the walls of a tent. She had no dreams.

The next day the ground grew rougher and their pace slowed. In the distance loomed twin rocky shoulders marking the entrance to a valley. She urged Rebecca to hurry. At noon she stopped to eat lunch on a cliff overlooking a ravine. Rebecca wandered off in search of the rare grass among the rocks.

The ravine had only one entrance, to the north. The cliff on which she sat blocked its southern end. Something white flashed from a patch of grass at the bottom. While she watched, the back end of a doe edged from behind a rock. The doe was nibbling grass and couldn't see or smell Becky above her. She sat for a long while, enjoying the sight, when a noise like thunder caused her to glance up.

Further down the ravine, rolling toward the deer on muscular legs, was a large catlike creature. Similar to a lioness but smaller, it had yellow triangular eyes and two fangs curving beneath its jaw. It stopped and roared again. The deer tried frantically to climb the rock walls, racing from side to side. But the beast knew its prey was trapped and like other cats paused to watch it, licking its chops and switching its long tail. Again it moved slowly forward.

"Help!" Becky cried. "O help!" The beast looked up once, then ignored the small intruder. No one was near. What could she do? She looked around for a rock to throw and saw some halfway down the cliff. It looked pretty steep. She'd have to be careful getting down. For a fraction of a second part of her mind said, "Don't! Go on to the First Ones. You're too important to risk your neck."

The lion was now within ten yards of the cliff and the deer cowering against one wall. Becky managed to crawl down to the rocks, scraping an elbow. She picked up one the size of a grapefruit and heaved it at the predator. It bounced to one side as the cat nimbly leaped back, growled at her and focussed again on the deer. It crouched to spring.

Without thinking, Becky stepped forward, and the ground moved under her. With a rumble the pile of rocks gave way and she found herself riding them toward the ravine floor. Miraculously, no rocks rolled on her, and except for one bad knock she was unhurt. It took some moments for the dust to clear. She saw the tail of the attacker disappear around a bend.

She scrambled to her feet and looked around. "The doe!" she shouted. "She's under the rocks!" Frantically she started lifting stones, though it was obviously no use.

A pebble clicked to her right and she looked up. There, stepping out from behind a boulder against the side of the ravine, was the doe, ears quivering and wide-eyed. Becky sat down and laughed from sheer relief. Behind the mother two fawns balanced on their long legs. The first was tan with white spots, but the second—she caught her breath—was pure white with large black eyes and two small bumps for antlers. With great dignity the mother led the little procession out of the ravine, not once looking back till at the bend. There she paused, her eyes dark and liquid. Then at one bound the three disappeared.

Becky found the cliff couldn't be climbed. She walked north out of the ravine and bent east until she found an easier slope. Rebecca greeted her eagerly, sniffing her elbow. Only then did Becky notice the smear of blood. It occurred to her that this had been a second trial. The thought gave her confidence. She even began to feel proud of saving the deer, until she remembered she'd done nothing but start a rockslide. "Luck!" she thought. "Still, I didn't run away from trouble."

As the sun lowered, they passed the high entrance to the valley and up a rocky road between walls steep enough to be those of a canyon. The sun slipped over the rim and a long shadow rushed toward them, swallowing the road. They passed three caves in the dusk, but Becky had no desire to disturb those who might dwell within. She shivered. The caves reminded her of black, toothless mouths. Instead she made a fire under an overhanging rock, rolling herself up in her blanket. She woke up cold in the middle of the night and noticed how bright the stars shone. When she woke again in the morning, she was warm. Over her own blanket lay a heavier one, woven from tough fibers. She wondered if the First Ones had given it to her.

With silent thanks she folded it and put it aside, still feeling no desire to approach the caves. Sharing the last of her dried fruit with Rebecca, she said, "I know you're hungry, old girl." She looked about at the bare rocks. Tonight she must find hospitality or they'd both lie out hungry. Last, she bathed her elbow in the rushing stream that lined the bottom of this valley. It was stiff, but not swollen.

All day they climbed the rocky road. At first it seemed to go on forever, but in early afternoon she glimpsed the end: a streaming froth of water fell into the valley miles ahead. Once she looked back and saw two men with beards—one white and one salt-and-pepper—watching her from the mouths of caves. The hairs on her arms rose. "Go back before it's too late!" a small, fearful voice croaked in her head. She remembered the blanket, however, and the fear dwindled. But she walked faster.

It was midafternoon before she reached the falls. The roar was deafening. Below them a large pool foamed and churned. She dared not swim in it, but waded in an eddy further down. The rocks here were green with moss, and Rebecca gave her full attention to a patch of lush grass.

Here the track became a narrow, rocky path zig-zagging up beside the waterfall. It was too steep for a horse. For a long time Becky wondered if she should turn back and seek some other way. At last she said sadly, "Rebecca, be a good girl and wait for me here." She patted the mare's neck, and taking her pack, started up the wet and slippery rocks. At first her progress was good, and her spirits rose. She enjoyed looking back. Soon she could see the valley entrance, then the lands beyond, stretching to the blue horizon. She even caught a gleam of the river they'd crossed the first day.

Gradually the path steepened. Whole sections had been washed out by rain, and she had to creep from rock to rock. Climbing demanded all her attention. At one resting place she looked down and grew dizzy. It was impossible to climb down the way she'd come up. That was obvious. Also, her pack was now a nuisance. First, she emptied it of everything she didn't really need. Finally, she pocketed her flute and flint and steel and dropped the pack and blanket. She watched them turn and flutter down the falls. She knew she had to hurry, for the sun was about to disappear beyond the top. Yet she couldn't go too fast, either, for fear of slipping.

Rock by rock, she pulled herself up, pausing at each step to plan the next. Fortunately, the way was marked by faint X's chipped in the limestone. But it looked as if no one had climbed this way for years. At the next resting place, she glanced up. Her heart sank. A hundred yards to go—straight up! And the sun was good for only another ten minutes. Doggedly, she moved on. Light slipped off the rocks little by little. The shadows grew larger. Finally, at one rush, a cool shadow swallowed the cliff face. She pulled herself over a ledge and lay panting. She could go no further.

Yet, as her eyes adjusted to the twilight, she spied a dark opening in the rock ahead of her. It looked man-made. She stood up and edged her way into the blackness—one step, two steps. Her foot met something solid. She reached forward but touched nothing except air. Lifting her foot, she found a low ledge. She stepped up on this and scraped her other toe forward. Blocked again. Then up, and another ledge. These were stairs carved into the rock! Stooping to hands and knees, she felt her way up them, remembering stories of people who climbed stairs in the dark which ended nowhere and sent them plummeting to their deaths. The stairs curved steadily right as they climbed, spiraling up into the rock. A draft moved past her. It must have an exit somewhere. The darkness was eerie, yet to one who had been hanging over a cliff for hours the solid stone on all sides felt good.

The air grew a shade lighter. Now she could make out the shape of the stairs, carved in solid rock. Far overhead shone a tiny rectangle of sky. She climbed faster. At long last, panting, she emerged. She was on a wide heath covered with gorse and white heather, about which bees buzzed in bright circles. The heath stretched for miles under a westering sun. She turned around and looked back down the long valley she had climbed. Rebecca and the pool were hidden by the overhang, and much of the valley lay in shadow, but the distance glittered in the light from the sinking sun. She turned again and walked toward it. After a time she heard a wild cry, answered by three others. Before her the heath fell away to an edge of bright silver: the ocean.

She paused long at the sight. The three gulls above her laughed again. At that she ran down the sloping heath, bounding from one springy hillock to another. Two or three times she threw herself down and rolled for sheer joy. Out of breath at last, she lay and looked up at the sky gradually turning gold. She was on the edge of cliffs warm and golden in the setting sun. She turned and gazed at the beach below, at the gulls, and at the reddening disc, entirely forgetful of the coming night.

"Each time it is beautiful, and each time it is different," said a voice behind her. Becky sat up to find an old man standing over her leaning on a staff. He wore a simple white robe, and his beard, more white than black, fell like a waterfall to his knees. He looked down, smiling, his eyes blue against the lighter blue of the sky.

"Come, my daughter," he said. "It will soon be night and you have met severe trials. You must be hungry and tired."

Without replying, Becky stood up. Each word had

gone through her like a shaft of sun. She felt she'd known this man all her life. He turned and walked along the edge of the cliff about a quarter mile. She followed. He disappeared over the edge. In a moment she caught sight of him again on a nearly invisible path clinging to the cliff face. In a few yards it widened to a comfortable ledge. There the old man vanished into the rock. Becky climbed down after him and found the entrance to a cave. Its interior glowed red in the glare of the sun. Inside, he was gathering seaweed for a fire.

Perfectly at ease, she asked, "Are you a First One?" Without turning he answered, "Yes, I am a First One—Aegos is my name. We have been expecting you."

"Rebecca, my horse—" she started to explain.

"She is already housed for the night," he interrupted her, smiling mysteriously.

The cave contained very little: an alcove in the wall served as a bed, two blankets folded at its foot. A jug stood by a raised hearth where the old man blew on a tiny flame. A light far above revealed a blackened chimney hole. A table supported a leather-bound book and three scrolls glowing yellow in the sun. Above the table a mural covered the wall in red, blue, and green; the bands of color formed an elaborate maze. The old man took a loaf and a bowl of something from a shelf. Just inside the cave mouth hung a wooden door suspended from stone hinges. He motioned for Becky to take the only chair. He was barefoot.

Aegos said nothing while he cut the bread with a stone knife and put the contents of the bowl in a pan.

Then he scraped hot coals together and slid the pan over them. In a few minutes he handed Becky a chunk of bread and a bowl of hot, savory stew. He poured her a cup of water, and after taking a pinch of bread himself, sat back and watched her eat. The stew steamed with a dozen delicious smells she tried in vain to identify. It was a meal in itself.

"What's in it?" she asked, mopping up the last of it with bread—the only eating implement besides her fingers.

"Heather, roots, nuts—many things." He waved toward the back of the cave where dried plants hung from the ceiling. The sun set while they ate and a cool breeze sprang up. Aegos shut the door and piled peat turves in the fire. Soon the whole cave was warm and snug, lit by a rosy glow.

Becky felt at home. Entirely comfortable, she felt no need to talk, even to ask about tomorrow. She somehow knew her questions would be answered in good time. Meanwhile the fire was pleasant and the heavy, wild smell of the peat made her sleepy. She yawned.

As if reading her thoughts, Aegos said, "Tomorrow I will take you to the Council in the Cave of Many Colors. There you shall talk with Menos. Now you must rest, for you have much before you." He pointed to the bed. Becky stretched herself on the stone ledge. Aegos covered her with one blanket, folding the other to a pillow. While she drifted to sleep, she saw him sit down cross-legged before the fire and stare intently into its bright depths.

·   *The Prophecy*   ·

The next morning she woke to the flashing of the
sea and the screaming of gulls. The door wide open.
Aegos was nowhere to be seen. Water lights played off
the ceiling and a noisy gull nearly swooped in.
Breakfast—a chunk of bread, a mug of milk, and a lump
of yellow butter—had been left for her on the hearth. As
she reached for it, a flurry of wings filled the entrance
and a gull landed on her shoulder with a squawk. He
wore a necklace of tiny shells and blinked solemnly,
nodding toward the bread. She laughed, gave him part,
and he flapped out into the bright morning.

   After breakfast she followed stone steps down to a
pebble beach. There she bathed in the ocean, clothes
and all, while the gull swooped around her in circles.
When she climbed back to the heather, letting wind and
sun dry her, he followed. Soon, she saw Aegos striding
toward her.

   "I have been with Menos." He smiled. "He is

ready to receive you at the Council. I hope Squall-
feather left you some breakfast!''

''Enough,'' Becky smiled back.

Holding up a strip of cloth, he apologized, ''I'm
afraid you'll have to be blindfolded on the way to the
hidden valley. Are you ready?'' She nodded.

Gently he tied the cloth over her eyes and took her
by the hand. It was rough going at first and she guessed
they must be walking north, since there cliffs rose
above the heath in a rocky face broken by narrow
ravines. Aegos patiently helped her over rocks. Twice it
grew dark and cool and their footsteps echoed as they
walked through tunnels. After an hour Aegos stopped.
He removed the blindfold.

They were standing in the mouth of a cave looking
north over a valley. It was not the same valley she'd
walked up yesterday. Surrounded by high limestone
cliffs, it was almost square. Trees crowded the tops.
Down the northern cliff fell a shimmer of blue-green
water. Below them, in the center, a grove of beeches
stood shoulder to shoulder around an emerald pool. The
cliffs were honeycombed with caves.

In front of each cave, some sitting, others standing, were men and women. The men's beards and the
women's hair grew to the waist. They wore identical
white robes. Some, noticing Becky, turned and climbed
toward the waterfall; others remained motionless. She
counted three centaurs, all of them at least as old as
Scopas.

All this she saw in a moment. But there was another element she noticed only after a minute or two. Whether it was the effect of sun on limestone or something in the air itself, she was not sure. The light was both brighter and easier on her eyes. It had weight, a palpable texture, as in old paintings. It brought clarity and a sense of great calm, yet within it was that movement, that music just beyond hearing she'd felt during the centaurs' Silence. The air here was sheer pleasure to breathe. If she had any fears of the First Ones, they fled, puny and ridiculous in that splendid light. The emerald falls winked at her from across the valley.

The sense of pleasure increased as they descended toward the pool. Becky knew she would meet Menos behind the waterfall. Yet that anxious thought didn't interfere with her enjoyment of each moment. Her eyes took in every detail. Even the feeling of rock or grass underfoot was a source of joy. As they entered the grove, every beech, with its smooth bole and translucent leaves, formed a universe in itself, a green galaxy which stood through all time—or, rather, beyond time. The pond picked up the reflection of each tree and gave it back to the clear heavens.

As they strolled, Aegos told her of life among the First Ones both in this hidden valley and elsewhere.

"Our life is simple," he explained. "Most of the time we spend standing or sitting still, tuning ourselves to that melody which underlies all being. The stillness is called 'contemplation.' A man or woman is most active when most still. The stillness prepares us for the Great Change that follows this life and restores us to that one-

ness of heart our ancestors lost—time out of mind—
when Kalendos sought the Thing That Is Not."

A bright yellow bird landed above them. It cocked
an eye at her and warbled.

"Like that bird," he continued, "we offer the
world in praise back to the Shaper. Our minds and
hearts go to the roots of all things and lift them up.
Some say we thus—with the Shaper—hold all things
together, that light would fail and the Warper wake
chaos, but for the steady attention of the First Ones to
the joy behind all things." A second bird joined the
first. The two sang a duet.

"In the outer world, man and centaur act, but they
often lose the light, and with it part of themselves.
Some hold to it more than others. Every eighth day the
centaurs, for instance, put aside their work and draw
together. They know the spirit is drained through the
repeated routine of work. On the eighth day, the spirit
can be refilled. They face the West in wordless song,
calling to That which made the world and lies behind it.
As they sing, they rest and listen for the music that
comes from beyond tree, stone, and star." He paused
by the edge of the pool.

Before them a woman bent over and filled a jug.
Balancing it on her head, she climbed back up to the
rocks. At her cave she turned with a smile that flooded
them like a warm wave.

"Our outward life is very simple." Aegos gestured
toward the woman. "We drink only water and eat only
fruits of the earth, with some milk and cheese. We rec-

ognize that many things can possess a man and enslave him—that the fewer things he calls 'mine' on the outside the richer he may be on the inside." His face darkened. "Alas, this wisdom, which each must learn for himself, is forgotten in the outer world. The desire for many things makes men restless and unhappy. One day, we fear, man's greed will hasten the end of the earth."

All this time a sense of awe grew in Becky. When finally they passed behind the splashing green curtain, it seemed as if she were entering a large cathedral. Yet she also felt as light and happy as a dragonfly dancing in the sun.

Once inside, she gasped. Across the ceiling high above her moved a shimmering band of colors—red, blue, green, yellow—mixing and spilling down the walls. Light bending through the green waterfall created a moving rainbow. Mingling with it through windows in the far wall was light reflected from the sea. Once more she heard the cry of gulls.

Standing together, their robes flashing in the colored light, the First Ones faced one end of the cave. All were still. Then, from among them, swelled a low chant. It resembled the singing on the eighth day, yet was different, as an organ is different from a piano—richer, and more various. The walls vibrated to it. In the middle of a growing wave of sound, Becky stood on a point, balanced between joy and sorrow.

It stopped. On a dais at one end of the cave, he stood. He was unmistakable. His face shone nearly transparent with a light brighter than the cave's. His eyes, at once terribly old (over five centuries, some said) and terribly young, fixed on hers and searched the bottom of her soul. She could hide nothing and had no desire to hide anything. He was Menos.

Smiling gently, he motioned for Becky to join him: "You have been long in coming, Daughter." He looked a second time into her eyes. "Through no fault of your own, I see. Alas, that Cavallos failed to obey our instructions! It was a folly that might have cost both your lives."

His face darkened. "The Rock Movers have gained much time by his mistake. Silver Garth may be destroyed. Yet," he smiled like the sun rising, "we hope it is not too late."

He asked her many questions: where she was from, how she came through the Eye of the Fog, and about her recent adventures. When she mentioned Rebecca, a whinny rose from the back of the cave.

"Let the horse come forward," Menos commanded. Rebecca clattered up to them, her head high. The colors flickered and swam over her white coat. Becky marvelled: could this young, bright-eyed creature be the swaybacked mare she'd met at Canters? Menos asked her to mount. He studied the two with a finger to his chin, then smiled and nodded. Finally, he asked about her trip to the First Ones. She told him of her fears in the grove, of rescuing the doe, and her difficult climb up the cliff. Menos listened attentively and congratulated her on saving the white fawn. "He will live to do great things," he said mysteriously. "You passed these trials alone; you have done well, Daughter.''

He turned and asked the assembled First Ones to stand with him in silence for a minute. At the end of this profound quiet he declared, ''Becky, we believe you are indeed the one mentioned in an old prophecy.

''Hundreds of years ago, my grandfather foresaw that Rock Movers would wipe from the face of the earth all talking creatures who could not hide from them. For many years he thought, grieving that this should be and listening for a solution. He knew of the Singing Stones—those places on earth where space dissolved before the Fall, where the First Ones had passed in an instant to other worlds. Across the shining heavens had the countless worlds of the Shaper been visited by his children. Near this spot, Grandfather knew, was such a Stone, where men had crossed in the morning of the earth to a world circling Alpha Centauri. Centaurs born in that world had crossed to this one and multiplied. They passed freely back and forth by the Path to the Stars.'' He looked down.

''After the Fall of Kalendos, the Shaper blocked the doors between this world and others, lest the evil born here should spread. Our centaurs were forever cut off from their first home. However, the doors did not close suddenly. For a few years they opened to the wise and good. Yet these had to exert great effort for them to open even for an instant. Sometimes the effort cost their lives. Soon none any longer tried.

''My grandfather knew the door might be opened

again if the right power were found. But, alas, all power had dwindled. He also knew of another place, called the Eye of the Fog, where one could travel through time into the future. This power the Shaper left to the First Ones—the wise and good among them—because such travel was limited to this world only.

"My grandfather's first thought was to move the centaurs to a future time when they would be safe. Alas, he learned there is no such time. Many are the ages the centaurs moved within, searching for safety. They troubled the greedy sleep of the Rock Movers' descendants and sometimes woke their youth to poetry. So the centaurs became wise in the future course of the world and seeded the sons of men with dreams.

"During his last days, Grandfather turned with renewed hope to the Path to the Stars. Meditating, he recorded a prophecy of how the Path to the Stars might one day open to allow the centaurs to escape. He died, however, without explaining the prophecy. Many years ago, as I saw the centaurs dwindling, I put my mind to figuring it out—together with other hints and clues. Slowly, I began to understand.

"So it was that I urged the centaurs to go once more through the Eye of the Fog to search the latter age of the world for one who would fulfill the prophecy." He looked straight at Becky.

He cleared his throat and with a resounding voice began to speak slowly:

> *Only one whose tree is torn,*
> *Half of blossom, half of thorn,*

Only one whose years are light,
Undarkened yet by grief or blight,

Only one to creatures close
(When earth is scorned, half heaven is lost),

Only one whose soul is sealed
In distant age, when world is healed

(By the blood that works all things
Crosswise to their hidden springs),

May work the Stones to conquer space,
Whose prison is all men's disgrace

(Though life for life be offered here—
Man's vanished powers cost him dear).

Then trust the horse to know the rider
And through the night and fog to guide her.

All eyes turned upon the two visitors.

Menos continued in a softer tone: "We believe the one referred to in the prophecy is *you*." Rebecca snorted and looked around at Becky. "The time is short—very short—for you to help the centaurs escape destruction. You must lead them to the Singing Stone, to the Path to the Stars."

Confused by the prophecy, Becky was stunned by the revelation of her mission. Was she to be lost across light years of space as well as ages of time?

Seeing her confusion, Menos dismissed the Council. The two walked silently out of the cave toward the beech grove. There Aegos and the woman provided a picnic: cheese, apples, and a still warm loaf of dark bread. Though it was noon, the birds above them sang as in the morning.

As they ate, Menos explained the prophecy to her.

"Many of the meanings in these lines are hidden. It took much listening to figure them out. I will tell you briefly what they are. The lines refer to one who has power to 'work the Stones,' to open the Singing Stone to the Path to the Stars. This person must be

> *Only one whose tree is torn,*
> *Half of blossom, half of thorn.*

The tree refers to the chosen one's family tree. He, or she, must descend from a mixture of good and bad ancestors. For many ages to come the good and the wicked of this world will be largely unmixed, though even now some of one kind have a tinge of the other in them. The good are not *all* good, and the wicked are not *all* wicked. But in the latter age, nearly everyone will find himself divided between good and bad. These two sides will war with each other in his heart. Thus the prophecy shows this person to be from the latter ages of the earth.

"The next lines are clearer:

> *Only one whose years are light,*
> *Undarkened yet by grief or blight,*

refer to one still young, who hasn't been weighed down by the sorrows of the world.

"The lines,

> *Only one to creatures close*
> *(When earth is scorned, half heaven is lost)*

mean a person who loves nature. After Kalendos fell, his descendants gradually ceased to love plants and animals." At this Rebecca shoved her nose under Becky's elbow and snorted. "Often Rock Movers are called the Divided Kind, because they are divided from creatures as much as from their higher selves. You are obviously not separate from Rebecca. She is, in a sense, your other half. Together you make one—or very nearly one. Even your names point to that. Your ancestors destroyed the union between man and beast, but you, Becky, are one of those in whom it is restored. You are thus a bridge over which the centaurs can move to an unbroken world." He paused. Rebecca was trying her best to coax an apple from Becky's pocket. A finch darted down for bread crumbs.

"The next words are a mystery," Menos continued:

> *Only one whose soul is sealed*
> *In distant age, when world is healed*
>
> *(By the blood that works all things*
> *Crosswise to their hidden springs).*

What this means is not fully clear to me. We know that in the last days the Shaper will send the Healer to earth. By a deed, a gift we cannot imagine, the Healer will begin mending the earth through souls who bear his mark.

"The Warper, knowing then his time is short, will do what he can to damage the work of the Healer. Yet the Warper will fail, and the Shaper, by ways known fully only to himself, will work good out of this evil, and at last, in great triumph, heal the world completely. The soul marked by the Healer will find restored to her many powers known to the First Ones before the Fall—as well as new powers released by the Healer's great deed. The soul will be joined again with heaven even as it is rejoined with creatures.

"On you I see that mark, though it is invisible to most. I have never seen the mark before. Truly, I am in awe of it. Yet there is much about it you don't understand, but will as you grow older. Still, it gives me hope that you may have the power—the Healer's power—to work the Stones."

Here he paused and chewed bread silently. The birds stopped singing, and Becky felt strange. She had never thought of herself as having power. The idea excited her. Menos looked at her keenly, as if he read her thoughts.

"No, this power isn't yours. By comparison to it, everyone is small and weak, yet it may work through one. If ever you think it *is* yours you are in great peril! It is the Healer's and the Shaper's alone. We don't know if you—or rather, It—can work the Stones or what it might cost you to do so. I, by myself, have never been able to open the Path to the Stars and have feared to put forth all my strength, dwindled through generations since the Fall. The next lines have always worried me:

> *(Though life for life be offered here—*
> *Man's vanished powers cost him dear)*

These suggest the Path to the Stars will open only at the cost of a life. *Whose* life is not certain.

"The last part of the prophecy is the clearest, thanks to your friend here:

Then trust the horse to know the rider
And through the night and fog to guide her.

Rebecca brought you—that's obvious. The trials you overcame with her among the Rock Movers and on your way here revealed a person with courage and one who loves other creatures, as well as one with the mark of the Healer. Throughout, the Shaper has worked to bring you at the hour of the centaurs' greatest need." He paused.

"But, why me?" Becky asked in a small voice.

Menos' voice was soft, "Why anyone? That only the Shaper knows—and perhaps Rebecca." His eyes twinkled. The mare nipped Becky's neck and grunted.

· *The Singing Stone* ·

Becky looked down at the finches pecking the crumbs. After a long while, she asked, "Where . . . is the Singing Stone?"

"An hour's journey from here," Menos replied, as a finch landed on his shoulder.

"That close!" she murmured to herself, but her eyes were on the finch as it hopped to his finger.

"Watch this!" Menos took a bread crumb and held it lightly between his lips. He then lifted the bird to the level of his chin, still balancing it on his finger. The finch fearlessly plucked the morsel and flew away with it to the trees. Menos laughed. In a moment, they heard it trill its thanks, and another flew down. "Here, you try it," he said, handing her bread.

Becky held a crumb lightly between her lips. The little bird (a red one this time) hopped onto her forefinger. She lifted it slowly toward her mouth. The bird cocked its head and eyed her doubtfully, then with a loud *cheep* and flurry of wings, flew off without the bread. Menos laughed again.

"Don't try so hard," he said. "Relax." Again she put a crumb between her lips. This time a green finch came down. She gazed at the sun-drenched cliffs. She felt it take the crumb and skirr off. It boasted of its exploit for a full minute of song.

For the next hour they fed the birds, and the birds sang for them as the sun shone through the shifting green kaleidoscope of leaves. For a while it seemed as if she understood their songs, as if they were telling her what it was like to be a bird, to live in that quick airy world of leaf and wind, sunrise and sunset—a world as distinct and all its own as that of the First Ones, or that of the centaurs. She looked over at Menos, who was leaning back against a stone, three different-colored finches balancing on his chin, his forehead, and his nose.

"Tell me: Why do the Rock Movers hate the centaurs? Why do they wish them dead?"

Menos sighed and the birds flew off. "Let us go for a walk." They strolled about the grove and he was silent for a long time. In the distance she saw the woman standing before her cave, arms raised. Faintly, she could hear her song rise above the cliffs in a beautiful, unknown language.

Finally Menos spoke: "That question touches on the mystery of evil itself. It goes back to the Thing That Is Not. After the first murderer fled into the East, the First Ones and the offspring of Kalendos made laws so that blood would not be spilled a second time. It wasn't, for many generations.

"But slowly the world began to change. One night a great comet fell to earth. There were quakes and floods, and the sky darkened. Then cold came, trees withered, and people first knew winter. Plants and animals began to compete for food and to kill each other. Some people started to kill animals for food and clothing. People knew fear for the first time and blamed each other. There were quarrels and another murder." Menos stared at the ground.

"A second time the murderer fled. But the wise among the people prevailed and adjusted to the change in seasons. They still ate only fruits of the earth, though now they must sorely labor after them. Still they talked and exchanged lore with the centaurs, the satyrs, the fauns—all the peoples of water and wood.

"Those of Kalendos' descendants among them knew much of working metals and stones. They used these skills only to make beautiful things, and the spirit of haughtiness was subdued for a time. Though the earth was troubled, the spirits of the wise shone brighter for the darkness." Menos looked up and a light kindled in his eyes. "Songs were made about the darkness, yet how the power of light overcomes it, and sometimes these stories were so beautiful they seemed to still the beating of the heart.

"More ages passed, when doom approached again from the East. The children of the murderers (whose names have been erased from memory) came, carrying fear before them like a shadow. In their guilt, the man-slayers had fallen to the worship of darkness, trying to appease it with blood, including that of men and women. Now they made artful pictures of evil—hideous to behold—and carried them before their faces. The wise among them were not wise in the lore of light, but of darkness, by which they enslaved the people, healing them only at the price of blood and riches. Over the years, these rulers fell out with each other and learned in fear to build walls of stone to hide themselves and their riches. They trafficked with the ancient forces of darkness—forces of the Warper himself—and made ruin throughout the land.

"But the forces of light burned brightly among the First Ones and they learned to hide from the Rock Movers—as the terrible newcomers were called. The First Ones befriended those among the Rock Movers who wished to be free of fear and blood-sacrifice. These they took among themselves.

"At last, though sick at heart, they learned ways to defend themselves. And so it went for ages, some times better than others, until the Rock Movers learned from their fear new and devilish ways of warfare and destruc-tion. Then the First Ones took to the hills, moving al-ways westward. The talking creatures moved too, and took with them the ways of wood and water, so that the Rock Movers grew fearful of going into the wild by themselves. Yet in rural or wild places nearby, the less fearful would still listen to the naiads' song or the danc-ing hoofs of fauns.

"As the Rock Movers multiplied, they grew insolent and haughty, and their lives were often violent and short. But this did not stop them from driving the remnant of the First Ones and the talking creatures into Britain (as you call it). They have projected their evil onto the centaurs, fauns, and satyrs and hunt them as if they were doing a good thing. Long ago they lost the true way of communing with moon and stars and all the things of this earth, as well as heaven. They feel their loneliness, but do not understand it, and by killing try to get rid of it. Yet it only increases." His voice softened.

"Not all are locked in this darkness. Some have good dreams and wander, in dream or reality, among the remote hills, where they watch fauns dance or hear the song of the dryads. The poets among them carry these happy songs and stories back to their people. Some refuse any longer to make sacrifice to the dark gods, but these few are usually killed or cast out by the others. Some have taken to living in caves with the First Ones.

"In recent years the hunters among them have waxed so bold as to try to exterminate the centaurs and other peoples of wood and water. The Rock Movers hate the beast within themselves because the beast has waxed cold and cruel, and would devour his neighbor. Therefore the Rock Movers hate us and the satyrs and fauns, because in us they see the human linked to the beast within."

He stopped. Birds sang in the trees. They sat still for a long while listening. Finally Becky asked, "But why does the Shaper allow all this to happen?"

"That is known only to the Shaper," Menos replied. "Sometimes we think we have a glimpse of why. Sometimes the Shaper may take what the Warper has twisted and make from it a thing more beautiful than before. Sometimes good is better for having overcome evil. But finally, only the Shaper knows the 'why,' and finally only he shapes good out of all."

At that, Menos stretched. The sun was halfway down toward the western rim. "Goodnight, my daughter," he said. "Tomorrow you and I must go to the Singing Stone. Now we must rest, for we'll need all our strength." Again Aegos blindfolded her and for a moment she felt lost, as if she were walking into darkness away from the light of paradise itself.

That night in Aegos' cave was similar to the one before. If anything, Aegos spoke less. She slept dreamlessly and long. Late the next morning, after bathing, she climbed up the cliff. Menos and Rebecca were waiting for her. He smiled cheerfully and turned south along the cliff. She mounted Rebecca and followed. The heather smelled sweet and the bees were busy at work. Menos' step was springy, despite his centuries. They walked an hour along the cliff top. In the exhilarating air Becky's anxiety evaporated.

Soon they cut inland and climbed a small hill toward a white stone. It was a standing stone, made of a smooth white substance, transparent at the edges. This one rose at least twenty feet. Menos moved around it to the east. He sat down cross-legged and motioned to Becky to do the same. His eyes on the Stone, he said, "We will wait in quiet for the first star."

Fortunately, Becky had practiced how to sit and

look at things. For a whole afternoon her eyes drank in heather and ocean and sinking sun. She didn't feel restless or bored. Slowed down, she saw into the heart of a single heather blossom a few inches from her nose. Time didn't move, she reflected. Rather, things moved through it as the sun moved through the sky.

They bestirred themselves for supper. Afterwards Becky saw why Menos was called the White One. His beard and robe now glowed white as the Stone—then, as the sun set, a deep rose. When the sun had gone, Stone and seer still glowed in the twilight.

The sky darkened and one star appeared. A fresh breeze blew. She wasn't sure she heard it at first. Soon it was unmistakable: a low humming from the Stone. It grew louder until the alabaster column vibrated. The note went higher or lower as the wind varied. Menos hummed with it, and Becky joined in. More stars appeared. They rose and ordered themselves to the humming. Earth and stars sang together in the fading light.

Softly Menos chanted in a low voice. What he said sounded like part of a ceremony, but the words were for her. "Now, Daughter of Man, look closely where the Stone joins the earth." At that, he sprang up and whacked the Stone with his staff. The Stone rang loudly and the humming increased. But Menos tottered.

"Quickly, your pipe!" he gasped. Becky fumbled in her pack as he slumped forward, wheezing. Then, slowly and simply, as in the wood, she played one note after another. While she played, something strange happened. A large cave opened at the line between Stone and earth. It grew large—large enough for her, then large enough for a horse. A silver light fell from it. Even more strange, the cave was there only when she looked at it. If she focused on the Stone or heather, they joined as before, and she was aware of the opening as only a blur. It was still there, all right, but barely noticeable, like a smudge on glasses when the eye focuses on the horizon.

"It's really there—or half there," Menos assured her in a weak voice. "You're seeing into another dimension, and your eyes can't put it together with ours. Don't try to—just focus on the cave. If we can only bring it into focus—" he fell back with a muffled groan.

She glanced aside at the old man stretched upon the ground. He was so white he appeared silver. Large drops of sweat stood out on his forehead. Then the light cleared, and she saw a figure like a centaur lead others into the cave. The figure turned and with a shock she recognized her own face and body. The rest of the centaur looked like Rebecca. She stood up and started to cry out, but Menos warned, "Don't say a thing! Watch!" He was barely audible.

The centaurs faded. She felt herself totter and fall. Her arms were moving rapidly, lifting her into light. She looked aside at them. White, long, and feathered, they beat up and down. With little effort she soared upward, singing a wordless melody at the top of her voice. The louder she sang, the higher she flew and the brighter the light.

She looked down. Below her, clouds of smoke rose here and there. Masses of people moved between them, roaring as in battle. Now and then she sank to earth to help someone hurt terribly by the crowds. As she hovered over his head shedding tears, her tears turned to song. And the song would pour as a light from her beak and heal the hurt one. In joy she would rise to the heights once more, singing and turning.

Then she was herself again, sitting on the heath, and the loud, wordless song she sang surprised her. She and Menos sang together, and their songs were joined like the two wings of a bird.

They stopped, and Menos spoke: "Go now toward the entrance, my child, but do not attempt to go in. We see the entrance, but it is not fully there." The light was fading from his face and his voice sounded thin.

She rose and walked closer to the silvery doorway, which already glowed more faintly. She looked in and saw walls on two sides. As she gazed, it seemed her eyes were drawn into the cave. The walls thinned and lights shone through—stars, in fact, closer than she'd ever seen stars before. The floor was paved with stars and she was walking in space. Before her, one star shone very bright, almost as bright as the sun. "Alpha Centauri!" she exclaimed. "I am going to Alpha Centauri and its world!"

Just as she said this, the star began to recede, beckoning like all of paradise. A second later she was back on the heath, watching the faint silver blur of the entrance fade into stone. Then it was dark, except for the distant stars. She shivered.

"It is cold," Menos said. "Let us return to the cave."

Becky had to support him as he shuffled toward

Aegos' cave. He was too weak to mount Rebecca. The seer labored for breath as he explained what had happened. His voice was tinged with sadness.

"It is as I feared—we did not open the Path to the Stars the whole way. Yet," his tone grew hopeful, "we opened it partway. What I could never do by myself you have helped me do by your singing and your playing. We have seen that it *can* be opened. And perhaps you—with the aid of the Healer—will open it fully.

"The Singing Stones have a will of their own. It may be they will open in these latter ages only at the greatest need and then only for one pure of heart. Today the need was not there, but the Stone did give us a sign. And that sign took all my strength.

"I read the sign this way"—he stopped and looked at her keenly—"the Stone will open fully only for one who gives herself entirely for those who need to pass. She must forget herself—and all other things—for them."

He looked down, panting. "I am not sure what the cost will be. I fear for your life. You must try this only if you are willing . . ." His voice broke.

"Anyway, the only chance for the centaurs lies here, with you. I do not know if you will succeed, but you must try. You must quickly return to them and lead them here, even as the vision showed—before it is too late! Six days from today the season of Leafwane begins, when night grows longer than day. The Stone will not hear you call after that. Even of old the Stones opened only in the months of light. You have only five days to bring the centaurs. On the sixth, when the sun is above the horizon halfway to noon, it will be too late."

They walked on a ways in silence under the stars. Again they paused to rest. Menos clutched her arm. His hand shook, but his eyes glinted in the dim starlight. "If the Stone should open fully to your piping, they will go." His voice was husky. *"But you must stay. Do not go with them!"*

They stood above Aegos' cave, as stars sank one by one in the sea. A shadow rose from the cliff, and Aegos quietly joined them.

"If they do go, will I ever see them again?" Becky asked, suddenly empty and weary in spirit.

"Possibly," Menos allowed. "At the end of time and times, it is said the centaurs will come from Alpha Centauri to quell the evil that lurks in the earth and put it down forever. If that time is your time—and if these are the centaurs spoken of—then well may you see them again. But first they must escape from the Rock Movers.

"Meanwhile," he spoke with awe, "here is a wonder I do not understand. Today in your vison you received two gifts to use in your own time: that of singing and that of healing. You will find they work together." His voice faltered.

"Can you tell me any more?" Becky pled, reluctant for him to leave.

Menos closed his eyes. He staggered and Aegos caught his arm. His voice rose in a chant, as if repeating something he heard. "In your time, or later, when the earth has been chained and desecrated, when man is finally sick of himself and the machines he has enslaved himself to, there will be a time of great troubles." His voice grew stronger. "But out of these troubles will come a greater good—so great I can't describe it to you, and centaurs—many thousands—may come through the Singing Stone and help the good. In that time the earth will be remade as it was meant to be, and the glory of it shall be a hundredfold for all the centuries of its suffering.

"And you, Becky—Rebecca—who have among us been joined with that half the Rock Movers fear and shun, who have become in honor a centaur and, by grace, more than a First One, will help make a way for the new earth. And when the heavens speak you will answer them in wordless song, and when healing is needed, or wisdom, you will have them to give. At long last, when you are tired and done using these gifts, ready to begin the real life beyond this one, I know for sure you shall see them again."

His voice sank. "More I cannot tell you. I must leave you. Through all the worlds, fare well!" He turned, a stooped, frail figure supported by Aegos, and shuffled toward the northern cliff. Becky descended to the cave in a daze and slept like a stone.

The Forest of Hardros

She woke late. While she breakfasted, the noon sun crept onto the ledge in front. A shadow blocked the light for a moment and Aegos strode in.

"We must go. Immediately." His face shone bright. He wore sandals and carried a staff. Squall-feather perched silently on his shoulder. He waited while she went down to wash in the spring. Then they climbed to the heath. High on a northern cliff they saw two figures sitting by a third, stretched flat. The two were chanting.

"Who are they?" Becky asked, a sudden fear at her heart.

Aegos smiled and spoke softly. "Today is Menos' day to go home, to experience the Great Change for which he prepared so long. He spent his last strength to wrestle with the Stone and now waits for death. His life is both complete and just beginning:

(Though life for life be offered here—
Man's vanquished powers cost him dear)

he quoted. "There is great joy among us." At that the bird gave a sharp cry and leaped into the air, swinging out over the sea.

Becky turned aside. For a while the tears crept from her eyes. But after a few minutes she felt something else: a strange sharp joy. It was like a presence, a voice without words. It reminded her that Menos had lived for this moment, that he was now far removed from the troublesome Rock Movers, beginning the real life for which this one had prepared him. The voice was gentle and somehow familiar.

She turned back toward the cliff. The chanting now lifted her spirit. Menos' last act was a noble gift. Would she be willing to give so much to try to open the Stone? Menos had feared for her life. Would . . .

Aegos interrupted her thoughts. "We must now think of other things." He thrust his staff into the sod. "I dreamt last night that the centaurs are in great peril. I don't know what that peril is, but I know you must go to them at once."

They crossed the heath in silence, Aegos in long strides that easily kept up with Rebecca. They turned south, and then due east in the hot sun. Becky broke the silence, "Aegos, what will happen to the fauns and other woodland peoples if the centaurs are no longer here to protect them?"

Aegos thought for a moment. "For one thing, they will learn to hide better than they do. For another, legend tells of a white stag who will lead the woodland peoples. Raised by an ordinary doe, he will not be a dumb beast, but will have the gift of thought and speech and rule for a long age." He smiled up at her.

"Will Targ and the Rock Movers make war upon them?" she continued.

Aegos frowned. "I believe Targ will not last long, my daughter. There are those in his city who would kill him now, so hated is he. If a good leader replaced him, there might be years of peace. Some Rock Movers might befriend the woodland peoples and the sacrifices to Phogros be stopped. This is a picture of what might be. There are other pictures not so bright. Yet, one thing is certain: Targ will not rest until he has hunted the last centaur from the earth." He lengthened his stride.

They were going downhill. A haze covered all the lands to the east. On their left boulders marked the edge of the canyon Becky had traveled up three days ago. Aegos nodded toward them.

"The canyon is not the easiest way up here, though it is the most clearly marked. The First Ones watch that way and help anyone who uses it—or resist, if they are the wrong ones." Becky wondered how the cave dwellers resisted. She had no doubt they could. "When you return with the centaurs, be sure to take this path we're on. Centaurs cannot climb the cliff," he added.

The way became rough and narrow as it dropped down the boulder-strewn hillside, and Becky dismounted. A faint path wound among the rocks. Toward evening, they emerged from behind a line of boulders onto level ground. To the north, she saw the rocky entrance to the canyon she'd entered four days ago.

"Memorize the shape and location of this boulder," Aegos said. He stooped and pointed to a hand carved in the rock. "This is the path you must take."

Becky was tired, but Aegos showed no sign of stopping. Halfway through the remaining hills, he stopped by a stream over which nodded a handful of purple flowers.

"Here we will eat," he said. "Then you must sleep, before we part. Alas, I cannot go with you." They munched bread and cheese, then Becky rolled up in a blanket and slept.

She was only half aware of what happened that night. She woke under stars to feel herself lifted in the blanket onto horseback. The old man's hair shone white, even in the dark. He whispered long into Rebecca's ear, and she neighed. Then Aegos stood with both hands raised while the horse leapt forward into the night. There was a faint red flush in the sky. Becky remembered thinking that they were going too fast, that the ride was too smooth. Then all faded into blackness.

Something warm and wet was moving against her cheek. She woke staring into Rebecca's eyes. "Where are we?" she asked, sitting up. The horse backed off a step, nickering in the early dawn. Becky looked around. Why, they were in woods not a half a mile from the village! The light was dim. How had they gotten there so fast? And how could she ride in her sleep? She stood up.

"Stop that!" she said, when the mare nudged her from behind. "What is it, Rebecca?" The horse stamped the ground and pushed her again. "Why, you want to hurry to the village—of course!" It was then she first noticed it—the acrid odor in the air. She quickly mounted and Rebecca broke into a trot. In a minute they were out of the trees. She gasped. Before her, blocking out the sun, smoke climbed the sky. Her eyes stung from it even as her heart sank. Silver Garth was burning. "Lala!" she screamed.

A short gallop brought them to the village center. Around them smoked black, half-eaten timbers. Every house had been burned to the ground, and all the trees cruelly cut down. The Listening Post in the square had been overturned and spat upon. Gouged in the earth beside it was the shape of a huge ram's horn.

Becky slid off and sat down on the Post, stunned. But the horse would not leave her alone, continuing to nudge her. "Cut it out!" she said through her tears. "So what if the Rock Movers find us here. It's all over!" But Rebecca was now pulling at her shirt. Tearfully, the girl climbed onto her back. They were too late: the centaurs were dead. Nothing mattered now. The mare picked her way out of the village, to the north. Only then did it occur to Becky she'd seen no trace of the centaurs themselves.

A trail led north. Hundreds of hoofs, wheels, and feet had cut a muddy swath through the grass—the Rock Mover army! Rebecca snorted and broke into a gallop. For the first time, it dawned on Becky that the centaurs might be alive. If they were dead or captured, the Rock Movers would hardly go north, away from Longdreth. Perhaps the centaurs had left *before* the enemy came. In that case, the Rock Movers were no doubt chasing them at this very moment. Something like hope crept up her spine. She sat straight and looked around, for the first time alarmed at the danger she was in.

She touched Rebecca's neck and the horse swerved left into the tall grass. A meadow rose to the west where a thin line of trees marked high ground. She put Rebecca and herself on the other side of that ridge, just below the top. Under its cover she could ride and still follow the trail heading straight north over low hills. Beyond those hills, she recalled, lay the first of several woods. And beyond these, across a river, a forest spread to the west. The centaurs had talked much of the Forest of Hardros. If they'd escaped that way they would flee to it, she guessed.

She rode all morning, keeping just below the high ground to her right. By noon the line of trees joined the western fringes of a wood, a half mile west of the trail. Carefully Becky worked her way toward the center, pausing every few steps to listen. Once there, broken saplings and trampled leaves told the story: an army had passed that way. Her heart nearly stopped. On their sides, wheels smashed, grain spilling from them, lay the gaily colored field wagons. She covered her eyes, then slowly forced herself to look.

An ugly ram's horn had been scrawled in dirt on one light blue wagon. But there was no sign of a struggle. Obviously the wagons had been abandoned before the Rock Movers arrived and smashed them. It was a reason for hope. Still, the sight haunted her. Cautiously, she followed the trail to the wood's northern edge. Across miles of open grassland it entered another wall of trees. Something narrow and dark wound like a snake into that second wood. Occasionally the sun flashed from it. It was the Rock Mover army.

She headed back west until the low ridge again hid her from view, then guided Rebecca north. At last, the sun setting, they entered the fringe of the second wood. This one was mostly pine, and the needles muffled Rebecca's hoofs. As the light waned a harsh cry rang out from the center. It was answered somewhere to the east. Becky dismounted and crept silently from tree to tree. Before long she caught a gleam of fire and smelled meat cooking. She hunkered down in shadow until the last sunlight was gone. In deep dusk she eased herself closer.

Many forms passed among the trees. Commands, curses, and rough laughs filled the air. From the gleam of metal and dark silhouette of a chariot, she guessed they were heavily armed. She was about to turn back when two figures paused near the bush she was in. She held her breath. They were both nearly naked, their hair tied in braids and their bodies painted two different colors.

"So, it is settled. We will move out before dawn to chase the beasts from the forest," one stated.

"Yes, they can't escape us this time!" the other sneered and grasped a crooked knife tied to his waist. "They're too many to hide. The archers will flush them out and the spearmen slaughter them under the forest eaves." He snickered nastily and pointed to a group around a campfire. "It's good we put the fear of fire into these dogs or they'd never go into the woods after centaurs.'' The other laughed too, clapping him on the shoulder as they walked out of earshot.

"Priests of Phogros!" Becky shuddered. This was no small war party on a raid, but a full-fledged army. She had to find the centaurs quickly. This time the Rock Movers were prepared to finish them off for sure. A sharp scream shattered the air, followed by a roar of laughter. A man leaped up from a group of four and ran past her, gibbering. One of the four waved a red hot branding iron.

"Haw!" he shouted after him, "Now you're a soldier of the Ram forever."

The stars were out when she rejoined Rebecca. She led her west, out of the grove, and quietly across the stream on its northern edge. As they climbed the far bank another scream trailed from the wood, followed by a second roar. Rebecca leaped forward over the grasslands, Becky clinging to her warm neck. A quarter moon had fattened again and was coasting from cloud to cloud, revealing a dark line to the north: the edge of the Forest of Hardros. Becky crossed her fingers that no Rock Mover had seen them leave the wood.

They reached the forest eaves in an hour. While Rebecca panted under them, exhausted, her rider called out, "Cavallos! Centaurs! It's me, Becky." In the heavy silence she heard only the horse's labored breathing. She too was tired and hungry, but they must find the centaurs if it took all night. She rode a stone's throw west, stopped and called again. Nothing. An hour of this reduced her voice to a whisper, before a shadow split from a tree and a shape sidled up.

"It's Flimnos," the shadow spoke. "Come under the trees." Becky cried out with relief and Rebecca snorted for joy as they followed him into the dark. He stopped and waited a moment for their eyes to adjust. Even then, he was barely visible, his face and chest smeared with soot. They went on. The forest was ancient and left to grow wild. With difficulty they pushed through the overhanging branches and vines. There were no paths.

At last, Flimnos paused and gave the cry of an owl. A ghostly hoot answered him. They were shortly surrounded in the dark by other silent ones. Soon they entered a moonlit clearing filled with familiar shapes. With a shout the centaurs dropped what they were doing and crowded around in glad surprise.

Cavallos smothered Becky in a hug. "Brave one!" he choked. "How glad we are you're safe!"

"Have you seen Menos?" asked another.

"Has he shown you the Singing Stone?" asked a third.

"Not now," Cavallos fended them off. "All in good time. She needs to eat."

Lala squeezed through the crowd and they hugged each other again and again. Tears glittered on the centaur's cheeks. "We didn't know what you'd do when you found the village burned," she said, then laughed and hugged her again. "We hoped the Rock Movers wouldn't find you."

"She must eat!" Cavallos interjected. "Are you hurt at all, Becky? The village must have been a shock."

"I'm all right," she protested between spoonfuls. "And I *have* seen the Singing Stone. We must go there quickly, within three days." But no one heard while they asked her how she had tracked them and if she wanted more soup. The whole group laughed and babbled at once.

"And Rebecca, old girl," Lala patted the mare, holding out a carrot, "you brought her to us." Rebecca whinnied, accepting the compliment.

As others fed the children and prepared makeshift couches, Lala and Cavallos told Becky the story of the past few days. Scopas' last message to the tribe directed them to flee to the western hills, but not by the usual route, where they might be caught in the open. Taking only what they could carry on their backs, he had said, they were to flee north, to the great Forest of Hardros, and work their way west from there. The open plain between the forest and the hills was not more than a half-day's journey and, once in the hills, the First Ones would protect them.

The people had received the message with mixed sorrow and joy. They were anxious to follow Becky to the First Ones. At the same time they regretted leaving their homes and crops. This regret was strongest in Applehame and Rootholm, whose people joined with Silver Garth for the exodus. The leaders could not persuade the centaurs to leave in the two days Scopas gave them. Rather they delayed a week, gathering their crops. At last they left, in a slow procession, bringing their crops and household goods along in wagons. On the morning of the second day, scouts reported six hundred cavalry and several thousand footsoldiers approaching Silver Garth from the south. The centaurs abandoned the wagons at their campsite in the wood and hurried to reach the safety of the forest. But many of the five hundred centaurs were young children and could move no faster than a walk. They had all seen the smoke from Silver Garth.

Becky felt a hand on the back of her neck. Cavallos smiled kindly over her shoulder. "What did the White One say, Becky?" She told her story briefly. At her description of the door in the Stone and the blazing stars beyond, the others stared at her in awe.

"Did you see the planet?" Lala asked wistfully.

"No, but I saw the star Alpha Centauri loom before me half the size of the moon," she replied. "But, we have only three days to make it to the Singing Stone. Menos' last words to me were a warning: on the fourth day, at the moment the sun is risen halfway to noon, the season of Leafwane begins and the Stone will be useless." The news fell like a stone.

"How can we possibly get there in time?" Lala wailed to Cavallos. The leader looked troubled.

"We might—just—if these fiends the Rock Movers don't hold us back." Then Becky revealed what she'd learned that day in the second wood.

Cavallos gripped her shoulder. "Good for you! You were very brave. But you might have been caught." Sparks leapt from one of the fires, and Becky recalled the red-hot brand. Cavallos patted her on the back. "The Rock Movers' plan is bolder than we thought. But we can make use of it. Come, let's call a council."

FOREST OF HARDROS

CAVALLOS' ARCHERS

CAVALLOS' ARCHERS

CENTAUR CAMP

PATH OF ENEMY ARCHERS

PATH OF ROCK MOVER ARMY

N W E S

GRASSLANDS

THE BATTLE
OF THE FOREST OF HARDROS

All the adult centaurs who could be spared gathered in the clearing. Their number grew as still others arrived from clearings close by, strange centaurs from Applehame and Rootholm. These gazed at her in wonder. All, male and female, carried bows and arrows. The whole made a very grim and warlike spectacle. Becky recalled the frightening pictures of centaurs on the walls of Longdreth.

Cavallos explained their situation and what Becky had overheard. His plan was simple. In a few hours, children and their mothers, along with the aged, would begin to move west in the dark. A few warriors would go with them, but most would remain where they were to engage the enemy archers and convince them the whole tribe was still there. That way, the main Rock Mover army would continue to wait outside the forest. If everything worked as planned, the slowest group of centaurs would make it to the western border of the forest and the warriors would join them the coming night. Together, they'd make a break for the hills. Meanwhile, the Rock Movers would believe the whole tribe was still far back in the forest. "Now, let's all get a few hours' rest," Cavallos finished. Silently, the warriors broke up.

Arrow and Spear

The silver moon was far to the west when Lala wakened Becky. The two were to travel with the young and old, who needed to start early. In a few minutes, the column was lined up. They heard a faint command and without a word moved forward in the dark. Roots and branches got in the way, and the company moved slowly, stopping often.

A half mile from camp, Lala paused. A single moonbeam played over her face and hair. "Ssst," she whispered, "I have an idea." Becky drew alongside. "Let's stay back here with the warriors," Lala said. Her eyes flashed in the moonlight.

"We can't!" Becky protested. "Cavallos ordered us to stay with the mothers. He said he couldn't risk our getting captured."

Lala's face fell. But she went forward obediently, without another word.

When the line stopped again, Becky turned to see

if her disappointment had passed. But no one was there. She called and a face appeared. It was Milatha's—a mother with two colts. They were in line behind Lala.

"Lala's gone!" Becky exclaimed.

"I didn't see her go," Milatha replied, puzzled. Again, the line started up. Perhaps Lala would rejoin them shortly. When she didn't, Becky worried. What if she got lost, or was mistaken for an enemy in the thick leaves? These thoughts preyed on her until she could think of nothing but finding her friend. At last, she turned Rebecca out of line and hid behind a bush until the others passed. Then she urged the horse back along the trail.

She was just about at camp when she felt a hand on her shoulder. "Shh!"—it was Lala, her white teeth flashing—""I knew you'd come," she said, grinning. Early light filtered between the leaves. She had two bows, her own, and one similar to that Flimnos had given Becky, which the Rock Movers had kept. No matter what Becky said, Lala was determined to stay and fight.

"What if Cavallos sees us?" Becky asked.

"The worst he can do is send us back to the others," Lala said, sighting along an arrow, checking its straightness in the growing light. Dawn was minutes away.

Exasperated, Becky shrugged. "All right. But you must promise we'll leave when I say so, after the fighting begins." She said this without much hope Lala would follow her. She felt both terribly afraid and tremendously excited. But she would not desert her friend.

The camp appeared empty, except for two centaurs who heaped wood on the fires and made noises to decoy the enemy. Lala and Becky avoided them and made their way north into the trees. The going was rough. In a few minutes Lala led her into a thicket of elders.

"This is our line. Nikos is fifty yards to our right and Lamnos fifty to our left." The leaves hung thick. Try as she might, Becky could see no one. Lala whispered in Rebecca's ear. The horse lay down obediently on her side in a little hollow.

"Now you're invisible, old girl," Lala said, stringing one bow and handing the other to Becky. They took up positions behind an ancient rowan tree three feet across. Its bright orange berries glowed above them while they waited, arrows nocked on bowstrings.

The waiting was the worst part. In her mind Becky went over and over the battle plan as they'd heard it from Cavallos. The Rock Mover archers, he'd said, would probably enter the forest to the east and circle around north of the camp. Then they would sweep south in a semicircle, driving the centaurs into the open, where enemy spearmen waited to destroy them.

In defense, Cavallos had led his warriors north into the thick center of the forest. There they now awaited the attack from the north. This was the line she and Lala had joined. Meanwhile, other centaurs had slipped even further north, ready to spread out secretly behind the Rock Mover archers when they appeared. Still others had taken positions to the west. Thus, if all went according to Cavallos' plan, they would surround the enemy on three sides. She wondered if the plan would work. If it didn't . . . She tried not to think of what would happen if it didn't.

The first sun poked into the woods. A bird call prodded her to attention. Leaves moved. For a second she saw a face. She lost—then found it again. This time she saw a whole figure, green from head to foot. He stood sideways to her, bow drawn, about fifty yards in front. He was aiming at something. She looked to her left. At a distance, Nikos was standing in full view, unaware of the enemy. She wanted to cry out—to warn him—but her throat was paralyzed. The green archer steadied his bow; a cruel smile spread along his cheek. Unconsciously, she drew her bow too. She heard a twang. Something struck the tree next to the enemy's cheek. Bark flew in his face. He yelled. It was Lala's arrow.

His own arrow flew wild into the leaves, but in one swift motion he turned and drew a second, aiming at Lala this time. Becky screamed and without thinking let loose her own arrow. It went wide, shattering against a trunk. The enemy archer paused a second, confused, seeing her for the first time. He shifted his aim to her. She watched, fascinated, her legs frozen. This was it. She saw his arrow flash upward into the sunlight. His bow sprang after it. He leaped sideways, clutching his throat, from which another arrow had magically bloomed.

"Eeeyahhh!" Nikos sang out in triumph. It was his arrow. In a second he was beside the girls.

"Down!" he said. "Keep low. And thanks, by the way, for saving my life!"

"Thanks for saving mine, Nikos," Becky whispered.

"And you for saving mine." Lala smiled at her, blushing. "I'm sorry my first shot missed."

Nikos grinned. "We all owe each other something."

Another cry rang through the woods. Another. Then countless cries—to the front, back, and on both sides. Becky lay low, an arrow at the ready, but saw no one. Twice more Nikos fired at invisible targets. Once she heard a long, tapering groan. Mostly, they waited in silence, sweating in the damp dawn. Finally, she heard dim, confused shouting and the crashing of many feet through the woods. This was followed by silence.

After what seemed a long while, she heard a repeated low whistle. Cavallos, Flimnos, and two other centaurs broke through a screen of elders. Blood dripped from Cranos' arm; Drakos wrapped it with a white cloth as they walked.

Cavallos blanched when he saw the girls. "What in all confusion—Lala? Becky?" His face flushed red and he frowned, eyes flashing. He walked slowly up to his niece, hands on hips: "Explain yourself!"

Lala looked as crestfallen as possible. "We wanted to help you," she murmured, glancing down.

"Help us!" her uncle thundered, "you hinder us.

By the tail of your grandfather, I ought"—he reached up and shook a rowan branch.

"Wait a minute!" Nikos broke in. "These two saved my life." He explained in detail how they'd shot at the enemy archer and drawn his fire. Lala winked at Becky, one corner of her mouth lifting a bit.

Cavallos grunted and paused. "Still, they disobeyed orders," he said in a calmer but stern voice. His eyes gleamed with a trace of pride, Becky thought. "They might have lost their lives. And on Becky's life, all of ours depend. Keep them here until I return with the others." At that he plunged back into the leaves.

Rebecca stood, shook herself, and joined them in a patch of sun. A yellow haze covered the sky. Becky sniffed the air. It smelled like fall, though the leaves were still mostly green. It was hazy, she thought, even for fall. A breeze stirred from the east, bringing a whiff of something acrid. All three sniffed.

Lala frowned. "Fire!" she said. "The forest is on fire." While they waited, the smell grew strong. The haze thickened and breathing became difficult. Between branches to the east they spotted a black column of smoke.

The ground shook and trees waved wildly as nearly a hundred centaurs crashed by on both sides. His face and chest black with soot, Cavallos stopped for them, panting hard. "Fly, while you can still breathe. The fiends have set fire to the forest. Aii, that we leave behind Hadrios, the High Leaper and Nimbos, the Nimble-Hoofed. They will no longer run in wood or on grass. We shall mourn them later. To the west!''

The sky darkened as he herded them in front. It grew hot, and soon they gasped for breath and their throats burned. Flakes of ash floated down around them. Twice they passed limping centaurs, supported on two sides by friends. Cavallos drove Becky and Lala as fast as possible. Behind them they could hear a roar, and now and then a tree exploding in flames. The roar gained on them as they stumbled through the trees.

After hours, scratched and bruised, they saw the leaves in front give way to light. They had reached the western edge of the forest just as the sun was setting, a dark red ball in the haze. They galloped well out onto the prairie and turned. The eastern half of the world was on fire.

One by one others stumbled out of the trees. While they waited, Cavallos told them of the battle.

About five in the morning centaur scouts had spotted a large band of archers moving into the forest east of the centaur camp. The centaurs took up their positions while the two left in camp did their best to make the noise of a whole tribe. Emboldened by these sounds, the archers crept forward, expecting to take the tribe by surprise. As they did, they were picked off one by one. Confused, the enemy archers retreated. As they moved back north, one after another fell to the centaurs waiting behind them. The rest soon panicked and scattered in all directions.

A group tried to slip west and were picked off by centaurs waiting there. Only the handful that ran east survived. This much Cavallos knew. The rest he could only guess at.

Outside on the grasslands waiting in heavy chariots, with thousands of cavalry and foot soldiers, the Rock Mover commanders grew restless. Where were the centaurs, they wondered, who by now should be fleeing in hundreds out of the forest? At last some archers straggled out of the woods to the east. Instead of victory, they brought news of disaster. Taken aback, the priests of Phogros had nevertheless another, more devilish plan. A strong east wind had risen, and they set fire to the forest. Where archers had failed to drive the centaurs out, fire would succeed.

The year had been dry and, in a high steady wind, the fire spread quickly through the trees. The deadwood burned easily. Soon the heat and wind was such that even living trees exploded into flame. A wall of flame rose to the clouds and ate its way west faster than a man could walk.

Cavallos looked over the grassland anxiously in the fading light. The group of young and old had obviously gone on ahead when they saw the smoke. His worry now was that the Rock Mover cavalry might have ridden west and be pursuing them across the plain.

In groups of twos and threes the warriors stumbled out onto the grass. Cavallos accounted for all except five. But they couldn't wait for stragglers. Smoke cloaked the night sky as the troop started over the grasslands, wet with dew. Behind them an eerie red glow along the horizon grew brighter as the night wore on.

About midnight they heard a shout ahead of them. Everyone stopped in his tracks. Again the shout. "Kentauros!" cried a chorus of voices. Their hearts leaped as they recognized voices of friends and loved ones. The warriors plunged on, and great was both gladness and weeping in the dark, as husband and wife, parent and child embraced. A shout of joy went up when they learned that Becky and Lala had returned. There was much anxious running about until all were accounted for. Then some broke into high, piercing wails for those who would not come again—for Hadrios, Nimbos, and several others. In the middle of this lament, hoofs thundered behind them. All grew still.

"It's Kamnos!" a relieved voice shouted. Five young centaurs pulled up among them. Cheering, the others crowded around. These five had slipped out of the forest to the south, well west of the Rock Movers' army. Yet they'd seen the glint of metal several miles to their rear. The Rock Movers had turned west, marching on the grasslands double time, just ahead of the flames, lusting with murder in their hearts for the centaurs to flee from the flaming trees. The five didn't know whether they had been seen. If not, the enemy would probably wait at the western edge of the forest for it all to burn. On the other hand, if they suspected the centaurs had already escaped west, their cavalry would follow in hot pursuit.

With this new reason to hurry, the reunited centaurs moved along at a trot, the weakest at the front. They lasted at this pace only an hour, however; the young ones were exhausted. As the sky lightened, heavy fog cut off the sight of the fire behind and muffled all in an eerie silence. In that stillness, Becky worried. Another day gone! Only two left in which to reach the Stone. How could they ever make it—especially at this slow pace?

At last, she overheard Cavallos speak to Senecos. "I can't understand it. We should be to the hills by now."

"Perhaps we are," the elder replied, "but just can't see them." A few minutes later, a guard galloped up and whispered huskily, "We heard the neigh of a horse and the clink of a bridle to the rear. We fear the enemy are close behind in the fog."

The news and the order to trot were passed quickly back, together with the assurance they were nearly in the hills. Exhausted colts were laid across the backs of nearly exhausted parents. No one spoke as they sped up. After half an hour, the fog brightened. A few minutes later they trotted out of it.

A murmur of dismay passed through the ranks. Looming against the western sky, the range of hills rose, still miles away. Two smaller hills extended out into the plain. The centaurs aimed to reach these first. A cluster of boulders guarded a narrow defile between them; but it was still a good distance off. To their rear, over the fog, a few columns of smoke were all that remained of Hardros Forest. In one day the Rock Movers had destroyed thousands of trees which took centuries to grow. Hopefully, the animals and other inhabitants had fled to safety, but their homes were gone forever.

While Becky watched, a line of shadowy figures appeared through the wall of fog a half mile behind them. Her heart nearly stopped. From the dwindling mist, in long and awful array, rode the gleaming cavalry of the Rock Movers.

A harsh note rang out from a brazen horn as the enemy sighted them. The centaurs groaned and stumbled on. Quickly the Rock Movers closed ranks and increased their speed. Hundreds of black horses approached in two lines, each wearing a blood-red battle mask. Red plumes nodded over the riders, and a red ram's horn adorned each black breastplate. Over a bronze shield rim each face appeared fell and cruel with the lust for blood. They banged spears against shields with a hideous clatter. Above the tumult rose the exultant shrieks of the Priests of Phogros, whose red-and-black bodies flashed in the rising sun. They rode in black chariots shaped like the fleshless skull-face of Phogros. Each was drawn by one black horse and one red. At the priests' cries the Rock Movers stopped and stood deathly still.

Cavallos turned and shouted to the centaurs, "Hurry! Make for the rocks." They were already climbing as fast as they could up the rising ground. But the young and old slowed them down. A mile distant, the rocks seemed to move no closer. Meanwhile, the centaur warriors rallied to the rear around Cavallos and formed a semicircle facing the enemy. It stretched right and left, a thin line of less than a hundred. Each nocked an arrow to his or her bowstring. To Becky's alarm, Rebecca stopped, snorted, and laid back her ears.

"Giddup!" she urged. The mare ignored her. "I know you'd much rather be in the battle line," she said, prodding her in the ribs, "but we must take the others to Aegos and the Singing Stone." The horse wouldn't budge. "Drat your cavalry-horse father!" She kicked her again, to no avail.

The centaurs made a noble sight, though ridiculously few against the heavily armed Rock Movers. On each centaur face, Becky saw a light of fierce determination, a resolve to fight to the end against all odds. Cavallos called out a high piercing chant, one she remembered from the Eighth Day, and all the centaurs took it up, faces radiant. They lifted their bows to the heavens, exulting.

"*Please*, Rebecca!" she begged. At last the horse reluctantly ambled toward the rocks. Becky turned her head to watch, eyes fixed on the centaur backs.

The ram's horn wailed a second time. The Rock Mover cavalry shouted and lowered their spears. At the third blast, they charged. Their long line moved together, ever faster, bending in like a sickle to surround the centaur archers. These waited, outnumbered, but steady and brave.

With a great roar they suddenly leaped forward downhill. The countercharge took the Rock Movers by surprise, and their line wavered a moment. Then the enemy laughed and increased their pace, howling like fiends.

At unbelievable speed, the sides closed. Just yards

away, the centaurs fired their arrows. Some bounced
off shields and armor, but most went to the mark, and
the center of the Rock Movers' line was swept from
their saddles. The few who weren't, turned and fled.
The centaurs punched through the hole they created,
still in formation, and wheeled to fall on the backs of the
Rock Movers' right. Unwieldy in heavy armor, the
cavalry could not turn in time. Again arrows whizzed
and numbers fell with a crash. The rest bunched into a
confused circle, horses panicking and trampling their
thrown riders.

Meanwhile, Becky saw the priests, who'd remained back in their chariots, waving like madmen. The
southern half of the Rock Mover line had recovered
from surprise and now swung inward, charging the centaur flank as these wheeled back up the hill. In a burst of
speed the retreating centaurs narrowly missed being cut
off by the Rock Mover left. Still, a few among the
enemy fired arrows at their exposed sides. Then, at a
fourth note from the brazen horn, the Rock Movers
drew back to regroup.

Most of the others, young and old, had by now
safely passed between the tall rocks and were winding
up a narrow trail into the hills. Becky was waiting with
Lala and a few others in front of the stones, arrows on
bowstrings, as a guard. The centaur archers thundered
up. Far behind them lay countless Rock Movers who
would never fight again, along with the still forms of two
of their own.

One of the centaurs had fallen behind the others
and was limping slowly toward them. It was Cavallos. A

Rock Mover had spotted the straggler and turned his horse. He bore down on him with a long spear.

"Cavallos!" Becky screamed. At her scream, Rebecca's ears twitched and she took off. The horse had been itching for battle. Becky could hardly keep her seat, so wild was the horse's charge down the slope. In a few seconds they were closing on Cavallos, who'd turned to face the Rock Mover but could not raise his bow. Becky drew back an arrow, but found aiming it impossible from horseback. Intent on Cavallos, the enemy totally ignored the approaching girl. So great was Rebecca's speed, it looked as if they'd pass right between Cavallos and the spearman and be skewered themselves.

Becky closed her eyes. The next moment she heard a scream. She turned to see the Rock Mover pole-vault off his horse on his spear. He landed with a thud and a clatter of armor. She stared in disbelief as his horse swerved and ran back empty. The rider, surprised by Rebecca's rush, had dropped his spear point a trifle. It had caught in the earth, vaulting him out of his saddle. He lay motionless.

"Brave, foolish girl!" she heard Cavallos cry in a weak voice. Rebecca turned and pranced alongside him, pleased with herself. He was deadly white. An arrow protruded from his shoulder and one from his side. He was bleeding profusely. Becky cried out for help just as Lala and five others galloped up, already surrounding them. They supported Cavallos to the safety of the rocks.

While others kept guard, five attended to him. He

kneeled and gritted his teeth, and they removed the arrows. Biana stanched the bleeding and applied herbs to the wounds. Last, she wrapped his shoulder and chest in a bandage. Even before she finished, Senecos ordered them along the path. Cavallos stumbled forward, supported on both sides. Already blood bloomed through the bandage.

"Good for you!" Becky felt Lala's hand on her arm. "But you were nearly killed. You shouldn't be so rash!" She smiled mischievously and winked.

Becky looked at her seriously. "I had nothing to do with it. It was Rebecca's doing." Rebecca whinnied in agreement. Senecos looked over at her, his face drawn.

"We cannot take such chances with you again. To the front of the line!"

Single file, they climbed between the rocky outcroppings that marked the beginning of the hills. Below them the Rock Movers, not yet tempted to charge the fortified boulders, split into two groups, the larger of which gathered in a ring—no doubt a council of war. The other was picking up the dead and preparing camp. The enemy obviously were in no hurry.

While they climbed, Senecos explained enemy strategy: the Rock Movers knew the centaurs had to stop somewhere for food and shelter. Their cavalry could easily track and surround them and bring up the main army to finish them off. Or perhaps attack again themselves, this time at night. The centaurs might have won the first battle, but the Rock Movers appeared confident as to who would win the war.

Death-birds wheeled lazily on large black wings above the battle plain. She shuddered as the horn wailed again.

The Path to the Stars

All afternoon they wound up the narrow track between treeless, rocky hills. As the sun set they came out on a wide, grassy plateau, roughly rectangular. It looked like an ancient ceremonial ground, long forgotten. Here most of the tribe wanted to stop. Cavallos was panting and needed rest. So did others among the wounded and weary. But Senecos insisted they go on.

"We are exposed here. This trail continues to the top of that rocky hill. We will spend the night up there."

Without much heart for it, the centaurs again began to climb. The way was steep and the trail, long unused, filled with prickly gorse and sharp stones. Around the bare top of the hill, they settled in. The night was bright with stars and a new moon, but cold. Becky shared a blanket with Lala under the poor shelter of a leaning rock. Rebecca slept standing. Toward morning the sky grew overcast and started to drizzle.

They felt cold and hungry in the early light as they

stood about in wet clumps, munching the stale bread from their packs. And there was little enough of that. The path disappeared on the hilltop. Going down the other side would be rough. Senecos and several leaders stood gazing down into the western valley hidden in mist.

Becky had not slept well because of the cold and because they had only one day left to reach the Singing Stone. She had no idea how far it was. In that gloomy mist, she wondered if it would do any good to reach it. She searched out Cavallos, who had spent the night in a tent of blankets. The bleeding had continued, though slowed down by bandages.

"I'll be all right," he said and smiled. "It takes more than *two* arrows to stop me." His eyes were bright—too bright, she thought. And he was terribly pale.

Becky turned and climbed up to Senecos and the others. His eyes fixed on the fog, the leader said, "Years ago a little-used trail ran northeast and southwest through the center of these hills. I guess it is below us now, though heaven knows in what shape! If we reach it, we can make our way southwest toward the coast and the First Ones." Again Becky stressed that they must find the mouth of the cloven valley where the hermits dwelled. The old centaur shook his white head. "The trail I speak of passes by the mouth of Cavehome, as that valley is named among us."

The drizzle turned into steady rain, cold with approaching fall. Slowly, in a ragged line, the tribe picked its way down the rocky slope. They came to thick scrub and thorn at the bottom, and it was a full hour before they cut their way through this. Following a dry stream bed, they happened on a stretch of fairly open ground running southwest. Though there were no signs of a trail, Senecos hurried along it. The trees grew larger as the valley widened. Sometimes a tree trunk or boulder blocked the way until the stronger attached ropes and dragged it aside. Once Senecos stooped and exclaimed as he pointed to the outline of a hand carved in rock. The hand pointed southwest. "The ancient northern route to Cavehome," he declared, smiling for the first time that day.

By noon the rain had stopped and the sun was trying to come out. While they chewed lunch—leaves, roots, and nuts collected along the way—Flimnos rode up in a lather. The others rubbed him down while he related the news. With the rear guard, he'd watched by the boulders all the previous afternoon. The Rock Movers, beyond sending a few archers close to test their defenses, had not attacked again. Instead they'd built a camp and spent the night in noisy rituals to their god Phogros. In the middle of the night, a sea of moving torches and a clamor of horns announced the arrival of the main Rock Mover army.

At first light, the guards saw tents everywhere. Soon a mass of men detached themselves from camp and marched toward the stones. Rectangular in shape, the mass moved slowly. It came on silently. In a short while the guards saw the reason for its odd behavior:

the soldiers were covered with interlocking shields to protect them from arrows. This formation—a phalanx—made them invulnerable to archers.

After firing a few useless shots, the centaurs had turned up the trail. There was no way for them to fight a phalanx. Flimnos hurried on ahead to warn the others. The Rock Movers were now only a half day behind. They had already reached the grassy plateau the centaurs passed yesterday.

That news ended lunch. The centaurs hurried on as best they could. An hour later, the rest of the rear guard galloped up behind.

All that day the tribe wound down the valley of the ancient trail. By afternoon, Cavallos again had to be propped up. Becky went to him, but he said little, saving his strength for the march. Biana walked silently by his side. In late afternoon the hills spread apart on either hand. Becky's heart rose. They were in sight of the cloven valley of Cavehome. Between its high rocky gates, the sun was setting in clouds of gold.

Becky pointed out to Senecos where the hidden trail began, a mile south of the canyon. But he decided the tribe should stop for a few hours' rest by the canyon mouth. Becky urged him to go right on, but the weariness of the weak and wounded made it necessary to rest and eat. The rear guard rode back along the trail to scout the enemy.

Again, no fires were allowed, and Becky felt chilled in the settling darkness. A low murmur of excitement rose everywhere, and occasionally someone looked her way. The news they were a night's march from the Singing Stone had spread through the camp. The centaurs were down to the last of their food—having abandoned most of it with their wagons. They knew they must now find the Path to the Stars or starve. Families and friends shared their last scraps of bread and then went to drink from the stream pouring out of the canyon. The water was more refreshing than most, as if coming from among the First Ones gave it a special strength or virtue.

Becky, too excited to sleep, stood watch with Lala. She felt a growing sadness that tomorrow by this time she might be alone. Indeed, she *must* be alone. At the same time, she feared she'd be too weak to open the Stone, or that if she did, the effort might cost her life. Worse, however, was her fear of what would happen to the centaurs if she failed. Lala, too, found it difficult to speak. Finally, she turned to Becky.

"Promise me, when you return to your own time and I am in another space, that you'll not forget us. I will never forget you."

Becky could hardly reply. "I won't, Lala—never in my whole life." She cleared her throat, then added huskily, "They say no death comes to those in the light from the Star of the Centaurs."

Lala's lips trembled in a smile, and she took from her neck a blue stone on a fine silver chain. She put it around Becky's neck.

"This was my grandmother's star sapphire. I've had it since birth, though never worn it till today.

Whenever you look into it, she always said, you will glimpse the Star of the Centaur." Becky pressed the stone to her heart and embraced Lala. Both stood there, eyes brimming, afraid to speak more.

A shout broke them apart. In a cloud of dust, the rear guard galloped into camp as everyone leaped to his feet. "The Rock Movers are but two hours behind us," Flimnos shouted. "They have not made camp, but are coming on by torchlight."

Amid the sudden confusion, Becky mounted and threaded her way to Senecos. Gradually the cavalcade formed behind him. Two by two they started off, unwinding like a spool of thread toward the rock where the hidden trail began. It was a half-hour before all had disappeared up that slope, urged on by Flimnos. The rear guard were the last up, after sweeping away telltale tracks. In place of these, they left many hoofprints leading into the canyon mouth. Hopefully the Rock Movers would think the tribe had fled up the canyon.

Becky followed behind Senecos and alongside Cavallos as they walked along the high trail, here close to the canyon's southern rim. Cavallos was very weak indeed—his wounds had not stopped bleeding. Now and then he whispered to Becky and Lala. A quarter-moon rose, and small clouds like white seabirds flew before it. As it climbed higher, it threw their shadows down into the canyon on their right. Just once, Becky glimpsed figures of two hermits watching the strange shadowy procession above them. When she looked again, they were gone.

"Becky!" Cavallos' hoarse whisper sounded ghostly. She nudged Rebecca closer to him. "You and Lala are sad tonight because you must part. I too am sad. If I—" he coughed, ". . . *when* I part with you at the Stone, I will grieve. But I want you to know what Scopas told me after you left him." The trail was less rocky now and leveled off, bending away from the canyon rim. Ahead of them, to the west, fog was rising. Becky leaned closer.

"Scopas told me that if we centaurs go to Alpha Centauri, ages will pass before we can return to help restore the earth. None shall die under its light, and in that world memories will not fade, neither shall time seem long or heavy. At the end of ages, we may return for the renewing of earth—which may happen in your time." Here his voice failed and he paused to cough. "At the end of time, we may well meet again. And then we shall repay you and all mankind for the great service you do us now." He put his arm around her shoulders and squeezed. Rebecca gave a long, pleased nicker.

"Never, Becky or Rebecca, while songs are sung by our people beneath the moons of Alpha Centauri, will your names fail to rise in thanks and praise to the Shaper of all worlds." His voice grew weak and he stumbled. Something dark dribbled from one corner of his mouth. His breath rasped and he said no more, but kept walking.

Becky felt panic. What if they couldn't find the Stone in this fog? It was past midnight and they had far to go. What if they didn't make it by midmorning? Or, what if they *did* and the Stone wouldn't open? She dared not think of that. She exchanged anxious looks with Lala.

They walked on, silent for a long while. The fog thickened. Finally Senecos paused to be sure they were still on the narrow track. Everything was wrapped in unearthly quiet. The heather and gorse dripped. Suddenly, ahead and to their right, muffled by the fog, they heard the deadly wail of a ram's horn. It was answered by a horn to their rear. A murmur of dismay passed along the line. The horns repeated themselves.

"We're trapped!" Biana cried. The murmur grew louder.

"Silence!" Senecos shouted, as loud as he dared. "These horns may be in the canyon." Cavallos said nothing, his chin on his chest.

"Come on!" Lala said to Becky and without waiting for an answer swerved out of line. The two hurried toward the canyon edge in the fog. In a few moments the dark shapes of boulders revealed the rim. A yard or two further they stepped into clear night, to be met by a scene both beautiful and eerie.

The moon, about to sink in the west, lit up high banks of fog along the north and south rims of the canyon. Over the canyon itself there was no fog. Winking up at the moon like a glittering serpent was a line of torches far below. It stretched a little east of where they stood and wound ahead of them out of sight. Again, the brazen wail of a horn haunted the night. Becky shivered.

"The Rock Movers have been sidetracked, all right. We're safe!" Lala said. Becky was about to agree when an answering wail wound out of the fog behind them and to their right. The two girls looked at each other, puzzled. A mile back along the rim, torches appeared out of the fog and signalled to the army below. A harsh shout rose in return.

Lala pointed: "We've been followed up here too. They divided and took both ways." The girls watched the torches waver into the fog and scrambled back to the others with the news.

The centaurs did their best to hurry, but the wounded were on their last legs, and the line seemed to creep, stopping every few minutes. Worse, the fog brightened, showing that morning approached. They heard the horn again, this time almost on top of them. It was nightmarish. Suddenly a dark shape sprang up in the fog. Senecos called out to it to halt. A hundred arrows hissed from quiver to bowstring.

"Wait!" Becky cried, and ran toward the figure. It was Aegos, wrapped in a cloak and leaning on his staff. He threw it down and put both hands on her shoulders.

"O faithful one, you've brought them—just in time, it seems." He smiled, but his face was drawn and grim.

Senecos lowered his bow and greeted the sage. Aegos raised one arm in return: "Hurry as you are until the fog thins. Then bend south along the cliffs to the white Stone. Becky knows the way. But you must outdistance those who follow along the cliff, or all is lost. I go now to the First Ones in Cavehome. Fare well through all worlds!''

He clasped Becky's hand and whispered to her. "Hurry for your friend's sake there." He nodded toward Cavallos. "His life beats very low." Then he vanished into the fog as if he'd never been.

"Lead on, Becky," Senecos urged. She rode the thin path through the heather as fast as she dared, keeping an eye on Cavallos, who swayed, his arms over the shoulders of two others. In half an hour they heard the deep boom of a drum from the canyon, followed by another and another. It seemed to Becky that between drumbeats she heard a roar of voices, but so distant that it might be the murmur of the sea. Then a horn blasted close behind them, followed by a hoarse shout. Thinking they'd been sighted, the tribe broke into a feeble run, but it was no use. A few yards and they slowed again to a plod.

The fog brightened as the sun appeared, a white blur above the horizon. They had only a couple of hours to reach the Stone. "Please, please hurry!" Becky urged them, under her breath. But she knew they were doing their best.

Soon she heard the familiar cry of gulls. Her heart rose. Before her the fog broke, and she caught a glimpse of blue sea in the distance before it closed again. In a few minutes they were out of it, on the edge of the cliffs, and all was blue sky and blue water. Without pausing, she turned south. The red sun burned through the east, and dew on the heather glittered. After hours of dark and dread, the sight of bright heath made her want to run and leap.

But once out of the fog, the Rock Movers would soon see them. Anxiously she turned around and was struck by the magnificent spectacle of five-hundred centaur coats glittering bronze, gold, and silver in the early sun. For a moment she forgot her weariness and fear. Senecos drew the tribe together into a compact mass: women and children to the center, archers to the rear. As they walked, these nocked arrows and prepared for a last stand.

But nothing came out of the fog. Becky's heart rose in a wordless song of thanks—cautiously, for they were not out of danger yet.

The heat increased as they rode south. There was no breeze. Becky felt a heaviness in all her limbs. Dread grew on her as she thought of what she had to do, and what would happen if she failed. Another few miles and the ground rose on their left. There, bathed in the morning sun, rose the Singing Stone. The sky no longer shone pink, but hot and coppery, and the sun, round and blood-red, stood nearly halfway to noon. They must hurry. She urged Rebecca on and led them in a circle around the Stone. The centaurs seemed to take forever to form a ring. She glanced nervously to the north for any sign of the Rock Movers. At last everyone was in place and silent, Lala on her left and Cavallos on her right, held up by Biana. Senecos nodded, "Begin."

She stared at the Stone, suddenly feeling very tired. It was just a stone, she thought, reflecting the coppery glare of the sun. The heat was oppressive. She could feel the sun inch higher up the back of her neck. Sweat trickled down her forehead. Time was running out and she had no strength. Who was she to try to open the Stone where Menos had failed? She pushed away these thoughts, but they buzzed about her like so many flies in the heat. She tried to concentrate on the Stone, but her mind was fuzzy and easily distracted. Some of the centaurs stamped and swished their tails, increasing her anxiety.

Out of the corner of one eye she saw something flash white in the north. Rock Movers, no doubt! They were on their trail and would soon arrive. It was all over. Her knees weakened and she started to slip off Rebecca. "Help!" she cried out silently, grabbing the mane. Again she forced herself to concentrate, to think only of the Stone and Alpha Centauri, to forget her fears in the thought of the worlds connecting. She tried to imagine the silver cave in the rock.

Just then she heard a cry overhead and looked up. Dark shapes wheeled high above them. Death-birds gathering for the coming battle! she thought, despairing.

She'd failed. She couldn't do it. There wasn't enough time and the Rock Movers were coming. Menos' fears were right: she was too weak. How could he ever imagine that she . . . Tears joined the sweat. And all these centaurs—she looked sadly at the faces around her—all these beautiful centaurs. All these that she loved . . .

She heard a sharp scream and looked up again. A

flapping shadow descended on her. A large white shape landed on her left shoulder and screamed again. Squallfeather! It was Squallfeather! The birds were gulls. She smiled through her tears at the awkward bird as he stared at her quizzically. The centaurs were looking at him too and smiling. How beautiful their faces were! For a moment she completely forgot the danger. Her heart moved out toward them in a rush of love.

All at once her fears didn't matter—her weakness, her failure, didn't matter. These were small things beside the love she felt for the centaurs. They were laughing together, fine and brave and free. They would happily die together. Something larger than herself moved through her and was reflected from each face. It was a brightness and a pain—as if she herself were being torn apart—yet at the same time a suffering infinitely desirable. In it she noticed only the look of love on each face.

At last—did she really hear it?—a faint note stole forth from the rock. It touched her from head to toe, increasing the yearning she already felt—a yearning both satisfied and intensified by each passing moment. A breeze brushed her cheek.

She waited while the music filled her chest and rose in her throat, barely audible over the Stone, then increased to a croon, and, finally, to a clear high note. The note rose and fell in syllables she did not recognize, in a language she did not understand. Yet she was carried along by the rhythm and the joy that surged through her. The tears still flowed, but they were now tears of joy. Here and there—first Lala, then others—the tribe sang with her, following the rise and fall of the music. She stared hard at the Stone.

As the sun edged higher, the Stone grew whiter. But that was all. She began to feel drained, as if strength were flowing from her. She recalled Menos' deadly pallor. This must be what it was like to die, she thought, feeling not the least bit of fear for herself. But her mind turned again to the centaurs. Her last strength was ebbing. She couldn't fail them now. With an effort, she roused herself. Then it was she saw Menos in her mind's eye.

"Your pipe—play your pipe!" he said. Of course! She'd forgotten all about the pipe. With enormous effort she freed it from her pack and placed it to her dry lips. At last she heard one simple note, then another. Gradually, the Stone grew whiter, blindingly white. It glowed from within. A blur appeared at the base, where it entered the ground, and expanded larger than a man on horseback. The blur sharpened to the silver entrance of a cave.

"There—" she called out, still singing. "There is the way beyond the world, the Path to the Stars. Do you see it?" Lala's hand on her arm assured her they did.

The two embraced and kissed one more time. Tears mingled on their cheeks, tears of joy as well as of sadness, since in the light from that Stone they clearly knew there could be no final sorrow or separation. In that light, they were together always. Becky pressed the pipe into Lala's hand. She knew she would not need it again and it was all she had to give.

With a grave smile, Senecos waved at her and walked slowly forward to disappear into the blur. Then Cavallos came over and embraced her without a word. Smiling, he turned and walked unsupported toward the entrance. Biana was next. As she held her lovingly, she said, "We shall think of you—and sing of you— always." She patted Rebecca.

One by one the other five hundred passed, each gazing joyfully at Becky or embracing her. Finally only Lala remained. She hugged Becky once more. They stood for a moment looking into each other's eyes. Then the centaur girl, her hair shining, stepped into the light.

Rebecca whinnied and started forward, but Becky, her heart in her mouth, held her in check. It was the hardest thing she'd done yet. As Lala's tail disappeared into the blur, the light cleared for a moment and Becky saw her looking back, smiling from star-riveted space. Then she disappeared again and was replaced by a star, blazing white—Alpha Centauri—Home of the Centaur.

The blur faded and only the Stone remained. Its light dimmed, and the faint sound from it became the washing of waves and the cry of a lone gull. She looked behind her. The sun stood halfway to noon.

A Morning Gallop

Becky couldn't say how long they stood there, but
after a while, without a word from her, Rebecca turned
and ambled north along the cliffs. Soon they spotted a
bearded figure striding toward them. It was Aegos. His
face shone thin and white and almost too bright to look
upon. Becky knew without asking that the Rock Movers had been stopped. He smiled and said nothing and
they walked back toward his cave. He disappeared
down the path, while Becky and Rebecca waited, gazing out over the sea. The gulls sang to each other in
high, exultant voices.

Aegos appeared again, with a heavy leather pack.
He spread out a cloth on the heather and removed from
the pack bread and cheese, milk, butter, apples, honey,
and nuts. Rebecca snorted and seized an apple from the
pile. Aegos chuckled at her: "It's time to eat—that's
plain horse sense." Suddenly famished, Becky sat
down to the feast.

They ate in silence. The food reminded her of how little she'd eaten since first visiting Aegos. Her stomach had shrunk, and she soon felt full. Folding up the cloth, Aegos spoke again: "You have saved a man's life in battle and led the centaurs to the safety of the stars. These are deeds of a great warrior, not to be spoken of lightly, but to be remembered in song. But now your mission is over and you must decide what to do. You are welcome to stay among us for awhile. We would be honored." He gazed at her keenly.

Becky blushed. "Everything I did seemed to happen sort of by itself, or with—" she eyed Rebecca— "the help of others."

"That is always true, my daughter," the sage replied." But those things just 'happened' because you did your part." He paused. "Now, what is your desire?"

Becky explained she would love to stay with the First Ones, but she really ought to find the way back to her own time. Yet if possible, she would first like to see her friends Rhadas and Neetha.

Aegos' eyes twinkled. "There may be more news from that quarter than you expect. Meanwhile, I shall guide you toward the Eye of the Fog." He returned to his cave for sandals and staff.

In the long shadows of late afternoon they descended the hidden trail to the plateau at the mouth of the cloven valley. The sun, smoking gold as it sank, shone on a strange sight. Scattered across the plain as far as they could see were shields, breastplates, helmets, spears, swords—all the equipment of an army.

Aegos pointed to an abandoned chariot. He chuckled.

"The Rock Movers fled in panic, leaving everything." The three picked their way between cook ware, harnesses, tents, and abandoned wagons. Birds pecked at scattered grain.

"How did the First Ones do this?" Becky asked in wonder. "You don't take up arms."

"No, my child, but we have a more powerful weapon than arms. It is hard to describe, but let me say this. The First Ones create a climate of thought so powerful that whoever comes into it—if his thoughts are wrong and his heart bent on a wicked purpose—loses his strength and sees himself as the wisp of a creature that he is. Far in the canyon, under the last of the moonlight, these fell warriors together with their haughty priests saw themselves like wraiths from which the flesh has fallen, empty jars from which the water has leaked. Each feared himself and grew terrified of his comrades. They stumbled back here in confusion."

"And the drum?"

"The drum was the signal to the First Ones to concentrate on the light in which nothing can be hidden."

"But what happened to those who followed us up the cliff trail? We thought for sure they'd catch us."

"When they heard the drums below, they turned back to help the others in the canyon, thinking they'd discovered the centaurs. But by the time they arrived, the others were already fleeing. These, too, panicked and fled with them." Here Aegos laughed and pointed southeast. "By this time, they've stopped running, but most will be too ashamed to look each other in the eye and will make their way back to Longdreth alone, thoroughly disgraced.

"They'll be surprised by what they find there," he added mysteriously. Again, his eyes twinkled.

That night they camped by the stream of the blue flowers. The flowers had fallen, but the leaves above glowed scarlet. Aegos toasted cheese on a spit he found in the Rock Mover gear. He also had picked up a bag of apples. These they stuffed with raisins and roasted in the fire. The moon had not yet risen and the stars shone larger than usual. A distant one winked and flashed at Becky as she lay down. It was the tip of the Arrow, pointing over the horizon. "I wonder if it is day or night there," she mused to herself. She felt one sharp pang of longing and fell asleep.

When she woke, Aegos was sitting cross-legged, gazing east. That day and the next they passed through fields and groves of the deserted land, now so familiar. Becky tried hard not to remember the days she'd spent there with Lala, Cavallos, and the others. Aegos entertained her with legends of the First Ones. Tactfully, he avoided the ruins of Silver Garth as they cut southeast toward Longdreth.

On the fourth day they came to a small river winding east among rushes. Wild ducks gathered on it preparing to fly south. Becky guessed it was the Temenos, the river that ran through Longdreth. Here it was still narrow and wild. They decided to risk the trail along its north bank.

"We are safe as long as we don't meet any soldiers," Aegos said. "No one else will stop an old man leading a girl on a horse. Still, we should be careful."

They walked side by side along the trail. The sun soared high and the water occasionally plunged down cascades, sparkling and flashing. Now and then the old man and the girl sang one of the ballads he taught her that went back to the times before the Rock Movers came west. As shadows lengthened on the ground, they sang:

> *In the green meadow*
> *By the dark waters*
> *Lived a fat miller*
> *With one fair daughter.*
>
> *Long though he labored,*
> *He couldn't keep her*
> *Grinding the flour,*
> *Stone upon stone.*
>
> *But ever her lover,*
> *The sly West Wind,*
> *Would visit her, singing*
> *One song alone:*
>
> *"Ah, how the flowers*
> *And dancing leaves*
> *Frolic before me—*
> *I do as I please!*
>
> *"Oh, how the waters*
> *Wrinkle with laughter*
> *As I pass over*
> *The miller's fair daughter."*

As if in response to their song, they heard a laughing, watery noise. They rounded a bend to find a mill made of logs. The wheel turned and the gears creaked inside. There were two donkeys tied at the door, with empty baskets on each side. They twitched their ears.

Aegos and Becky took to the woods, avoiding the mill. Over the next day they did this many times, skirting settlements and farms. Then the road crossed the river and ran along its south bank. On one of their detours, pushing through yellow leaves, they suddenly heard it—the wail of a ram's horn. The three froze. Aegos crept forward to scout the road.

He hurried back. "Let's hide here," he whispered. "An armed troop approaches. The Rock Movers have found their courage again." They hid Rebecca behind a clump of firs and then crawled to where they could watch the soldiers go by.

A man in a ram's horn hat and a blue cape rode at the head. He was handsome, not at all like the hideous priests of Phogros. Next to him, on a dappled gray mare, a slim girl rode sidesaddle. She fluttered with yellow silks. Next to her a fat old woman rode a mule with purple feathers at its ears. As they drew abreast, Becky shouted and ran out on the road. "Rhadas!" she cried. "Neetha!"

The horses stopped and Rhadas swung out of his saddle. Neetha jumped down from the mare and the three clung to each other, laughing and asking questions all at once. After a few minutes Becky remembered Aegos, and called out the old man and Rebecca. He shook the Prince's hand gravely and fixed him with penetrating eyes. "Targ is dead, isn't he?"

"Yes, honored father," Rhadas said, and bowed before him. "The nobles of Longdreth attacked the palace just after he had sentenced a number of them to death. The palace guard went over to the nobles' side and Targ hanged himself. Afterwards they pronounced me King. But how did you know?"

"I saw it in a dream," he replied. "And this lady?" Aegos smiled and turned toward Neetha.

Rhadas' eyes sparkled. "This is the Queen Consort to be—the Lady Neetha." Neetha blushed and stared hard at the ground. "And this is the Lady Calitha, her companion." He gestured toward the older woman on the mule, wrapped in yards of purple silk. She smiled a broad smile above two chins and laughed merrily.

Rhadas ordered his soldiers to fall out. Some spread a red-and-white pavilion over a plush carpet on the riverbank. Others prepared sweet fruits and cool foamy drinks in silver cups. One gave Rebecca a hot bran mash in a silken nosebag.

When the reunited friends had eaten and were stretched comfortably on cushions, Rhadas continued his story. "I started out from Longdreth as soon as I could, to stop my uncle's army from attacking the centaurs. I was too late, but fortunately I met them coming back in small groups, ashamed and frightened. They claimed magic had defeated them before they could find the centaurs, who escaped in the hills. Are the centaurs all right? I was on my way to make peace and hoped to find you among them."

All evening, till the early stars shone, Becky told

her story. Neetha and Rhadas looked at each other in silent wonder when they learned she was from another time and that the centaurs had escaped to a distant star.

"And they are to return?" the King murmured as she finished. "To think that all these wonders will come to pass in the latter age of the earth!" He gazed long into the yellow flame of the lamp while crickets chanted outside.

They ate supper, served on silver. It was late, with the moon glimmering on the water and a slight chill in the air, when Rhadas said, "Now we must sleep. But Becky," he looked at her hopefully, "will you return with us to Longdreth? We have much to do there and you can help us."

"Gladly," Becky said. "I'd love to visit Longdreth before returning to my own time." Neetha squeezed her hand. They talked eagerly of all they would see and do together. Aegos, however, declined their invitation, saying he must return west early in the morning. He looked keenly at Rhadas.

"One thing is clear: you, King Rhadas, have it in your power to rule wisely and well, to befriend the peoples of wood and field and to learn from them. You may, if you wish, create a peace such as has not existed for generations. I invite you to meet me at the ruins of Silver Garth before the summer leaves are full. I shall guide you and Neetha to my home beyond the cloven valley." The King and Neetha graciously accepted his invitation, confessing they were honored above all their people.

Then Neetha played the lute while they drank hot chocolate from golden cups. As Becky drifted off to sleep she pictured far-off Ack-Lonthea of the fragrant palms, where the chocolate was from.

The next morning, they woke while mist still hung above the river. "Let's ride before breakfast," Rhadas said, breathing in the sweet wood smoke. Becky noticed how his pale skin had browned since she last saw him. Quickly he and Neetha saddled up. Purple plumes nodding, their black horses reared up on hind legs. Rebecca snorted and pranced, rolling one eye.

"Race you across the meadow to those trees!" Rhadas cried, and was off. Rebecca started slowly, but gained on the other two. The three laughed at each other as she passed. Soon she was far ahead of them in the mist. It grew so thick near the river, she could scarcely see the trees as she raced into them.

"Whoa, Rebeck!" she cried. But the horse stretched out her neck and galloped faster. The mist darkened. "You stubborn mare!" Becky fumed, exasperated. In a few seconds the mist, chill and damp, hid everything. Just as suddenly, they were out of it among trees. Stars shone overhead and a half moon was about to sink in the west. Dark pines rushed by, wisps of fog curling through them. Rebecca sped even faster down the straight path. She whinnied again. Far off, she was answered.

Becky's heart caught in her throat. She looked behind. Rhadas and Neetha had not followed. She was alone again. It stunned her. Fortunately Rebecca's wild career didn't allow her much time to despair. All she could do was hang on breathlessly. In a short while the mare swung off the path and ran full tilt toward a dark house and rail fence. With one grand shove she was up off the ground and sailing over the gate. She stopped abruptly in the middle of a paddock.

With a shock, Becky recognized her father's car exactly where he'd parked it months before. Her head reeled. Were they really back? Was he still here? Had he given her up for dead? Rebecca looked around and snorted, as if telling her to get off. In a daze, she did, and the horse nuzzled her. Then Rebecca trotted to the barn and in its open door.

The sky had grown lighter and the moon was a white shell over the trees. Becky looked a second time at her father's car, covered with dew. Next she saw her window, still open. She walked over to it and cautiously looked in. The horse nut, her suitcase, and the rumpled bed were just as she had left them. She'd spent months among the centaurs, and yet it seemed she'd returned to Canters a few hours after she left.

It was beyond her tired mind. She climbed in, undressed, and crawled into bed. The hot water bottle was still warm against her chilled toes.

It was Charlie's big voice that woke her. "Hey in there—time to get up! We've got lots to check out today." She could smell pancakes and sausage frying and heard her father in the kitchen talking to Eleanor.

She sat up. What a strange dream she'd had—if it was a dream. She looked at the open window, then at her clothes. They lay on the floor, mud streaked and worn. Her shoes were covered with mud.

"Perhaps I walked in my sleep—out to see the horses," she mumbled to herself, still groggy. She swung her feet onto the cold floor and woke up a bit more. She marveled, as months of memories flooded in upon her sitting there.

"What a dream!" she repeated.

Outside her window Charlie's laugh followed his surprised exclamation: "Why Rebecca, old girl, you look as if you've gained forty pounds overnight!"

Becky stood up to look. As she leaned over the sill, something cold and hard banged against her chest. She looked down. It was a sapphire on a silver chain, and from its cloudy depths glinted the bright blue light of a star.

About the Author

Robert Siegel has spent most of his life in America's heartland, the midwest. Born and raised near Chicago, he now lives in Whitefish Bay, Wisconsin, with his wife and three daughters and teaches English at the University of Wisconsin-Milwaukee. After graduating from Wheaton College, he studied and taught out east, receiving the M.A. from Johns Hopkins, the Ph.D. from Harvard and teaching seven years at Dartmouth.

One of America's notable younger poets, he has written two books of poetry, *The Beasts and the Elders* and *In a Pig's Eye*. He has received a number of awards for his poetry including most recently a National Endowment for the Arts fellowship. An earlier grant permitted him and his family to live in England for a year. It was there, during holidays at a friend's farm and walking tours through the Lake District, that the idea for *Alpha Centauri* began to germinate.

Robert Siegel is also the author of *Whalesong*, soon to be a Berkley book.